I0627589

IRONIC

A novel by

Sebati Edward Mafate

"Ironic," by Sebati Edward Mafate. ISBN 978-1-949756-49-4 (softcover); 978-1-949756-50-0 (eBook).

Published 2019 by Virtualbookworm.com Publishing Inc., P.O. Box 9949, College Station, TX , 77842, US.

For my wife and cherished companion,
Vivian Lorena

AKNOWLEDGEMENTS

Like before, so many people were instrumental in making *"IRONIC"* a reality that, as in previous projects, pages would be required to mention them all. But the following are preeminent: Cathea Marie Walters, Ashley Green, and Ivy Miller-Jacobs, three wonderful women who helped me bring "Lucy Yvette Young" to life. There was also Mpho Mapoulo, Natalie Miles Mullaney, Tshepiso More, Louise Breytenbach, Mark Arnold, Talin Simon, Erik Hudson, Thato Chuma, Raymond "Words" Mafoko, Mothusi Kgakge, Brian Le Roux, Donald Molosi, Dineo Motsamai, Gosego Motsumi, Gary Stinnett, Randy Johnson, Amanda Texiera, Hugh Molotsi, Robert Mwamba, Cindy Lam, Sandi Hernandez, and many others. Thank you so very much for your unwavering support.

CHAPTER ONE

THE PRIVATE PRACTICE of Dr. Maurice 'Reese' Muhammed was located on the 300 block of North Lake Avenue in the beautiful city of Altadena, separated from the world-renowned city of Pasadena by a street running from east to west. The private practice was a haven for those who knew about it, because Dr. Muhammed never sent anyone away — medical insurance or none, rich or poor, black, white, Latina, Asian or other. If you needed medical attention and could afford to wait the hour or two it took to see the doctor, you were most welcome. Dr. Muhammed believed that, as a doctor, his mission was to save lives.

Now in his early 50s, Dr. Maurice Muhammed, a black man from Trent, New Jersey, knew all about suffering from an early age. Born to a single mother, he was at the tender age of three, and his older brother, Brian, was six, when their mother Doreen died suddenly. Since both siblings had never known their father, they were taken in by their maternal Aunty Violet, who had a brood of her own and was barely able to make

1

ends meet. The two extra mouths to feed, clothe, educate, and provide shelter for, did not help.

After several months, the situation only got worse; so bad that she came to the drastic decision to get rid of one of the brothers—the younger of the two, it turned out.

"Brian," she said to the older of the two siblings now living with her. "I can only afford to take care of only one of you. So here is what I want you to do. I want you to take your brother to Maurice Park. You know where it is, right?"

"Uh-huh," the seven-year-old nodded, wide-eyed, his stomach in knots; somehow sensing that something terrible was about to happen. He looked to the floor as he said this, because eye contact with his alcoholic aunty was never something easy to witness.

"I want you to leave him there and run straight home. You understand what I am saying to you?" She was stern, and the little boy had long ago learned never to question anything she told him.

"Yes ma'am, I understand," he said, even though he did not.

"The nuns who run the orphanage near the park, who are always feeding the needy, will find him and take him in. Leave him there, run back, and when you do, don't look back. You hear me, boy?"

Again, the little boy responded with a meek, "Yes, ma'am."

However, to make certain that her instructions were followed to the letter, she needed to make sure.

"Repeat what I just said," she demanded.

"Take my brother …"

"Ah-ah …" She wagged a bony finger at him, in essence telling him that what she was about to say was of equal importance. "After today, he ain't your brother no more. Now, what did I say for you to do?"

"T-take him to Maurice Park, leave him there, run back home, and not look back."

"That's right." She patted him on the head as she fished out a menthol cigarette, firing it up and then taking a gulp of cheap wine from her glass as she looked away through the cruddy window into the late fall afternoon. It was also to avert her face so the young boy would not see the tears that had suddenly welled in her eyes. The guilt of what she had decided to do had hit her hard, and would continue to haunt her for as long as she was alive.

Even to this day, some fifty years later, Dr. Muhammed never forgot the fear he'd felt when, after they reached the park, his brother let go of his arm and turned to flee in the direction they had come. How he'd tried to run after him; of course, Brian was way too fast and he could not overtake him. The pain he felt when the most important person in his life vanished around a corner – never to be seen or heard from again – was something that still gnawed at him, even after all these decades.

One of the nuns later found him wandering in the park—alone, frightened, hungry, and scared. He was then taken into the orphanage. Since he had no nametag or anything on his person to say who he was, the nuns named him Maurice, after the park at which he was found, and gave the last name Stevens. He was raised in the orphanage; and later in life, at medical school on a full-ride scholarship at Georgetown University, he converted to Islam, where he was christened Maurice Muhammed.

Later, after working many years at the Boston Municipal County Hospital in Massachusetts, he moved to southern California— Altadena, to be precise—and opened his own medical practice.

Perhaps it was because of his bitter childhood memories that he chose to be a physician. He wanted to help those who needed his help the most. His staff, and most importantly his patients, became part of his family. Whenever he lost a patient, which was something that was always to be expected in his profession, he always felt as if he had lost a family member.

Which was why, as he sat in his lavish office reviewing the charts, x-rays, and lab results he had just received about his next patient, he did so with a heavy heart. He knew this patient very well, a foreigner from Africa who had been coming to him for the past year and a half.

The prognosis he had for him was dreadful. The patient, a young man from Botswana who was bright, jolly, and full of life, had a brain tumor the size of a sparrow's egg. What was worse, this inoperable tumor was going to kill him in less than two months! What had started as a routine checkup hardly six weeks earlier, as the young man had been complaining of constant headaches, was going to end with the news that he, Adam Lebogang Mashabela, age 24, would be dead in less than two months. Dr. Maurice Muhammed dreaded having to deliver this grim news to the unsuspecting young man.

CHAPTER 2

THE RECEPTION AREA of Dr. Muhammed's practice, which doubled as a waiting room, was spacious. It was usually crowded. However, today there were only a handful of patients, including one whom the young Hispanic receptionist, Maria Gonzalez, and her colleague, Lupe Salazar, always made furtive glances at whenever he came to see the doctor—which had been quite a few times lately.

On this day, as was always the case, he was seated by himself, paging through a magazine. He was tall, black, light-skinned, clean-cut, and athletically built. This morning, though, as he leafed through the magazine, he kept placing it on the glass coffee table in front of him. With both long, manicured forefingers, he'd massage both temples, eyes tightly shut, clearly in excruciating pain. Lately the pain came in increasingly consistent waves. For Maria, this sight was all the more painful to watch. Each time she would bite her tongue to keep herself from saying something stupid like, "Can I get you an aspirin?"

She knew that whatever news the doctor had for the young, good-looking foreigner was not good. That much was clear from the way the doctor's expression changed when the results from the lab arrived the day before, which was followed by a swift order from the doctor to call the patient and inform him to be at the office first thing in the morning. *"No, no appointment necessary – just come in as soon as you can. Dr. Muhammed wishes to discuss the test results with you as soon as possible,"* was the somewhat ominous message Maria gave.

After rubbing his temples, the young man suddenly looked up, just in time to catch the pretty receptionist gawking at him with what looked like great concern evident in her eyes.

"Are you all right, Adam?" she asked with genuine unease. He had been to Dr. Muhammed's office so often over the past month that he and the staff had reached a point in their relationship where they were on a first-name basis.

"I am fine, Maria," he lied. He was far from fine, and they both knew it. He had a distinct accent that was not easy to place, unless he himself told you where he was from.

"The doctor will see you soon." Maria smiled as the phone thankfully caught her attention, for this diversion would help her to stop looking at him again and again.

Adam Lebogang Mashabela was a very beautiful man. He was gifted with the kind of looks that made people turn and stare, men and women alike—particularly women, who would always wonder who his lucky partner was. These were the type of stares that also made people curious as to what was going on in his presumably, equally beautiful mind. What was he thinking? Was he aware of his great gift? Did he socialize, and if so, who were his friends? What were his views on life, and so forth? The kind of questions people ask themselves when they encounter extraordinarily beautiful people.

He had been in the country for five years. Hailing from Botswana, he was born and bred in Serowe, the largest village in the nation with a rich history known to many as the village of the rain wind. He had immigrated to the United States via the diversity visa lottery system, where those lucky individuals obtained a green card to become permanent legal residents. Adam had seized this once-in-a-lifetime opportunity with both hands.

His greatest passion in life was photography. So, upon arriving in the United States and settling in Altadena, an all-American, beautiful and quiet city in southern California, he enrolled at a local community college, majoring in photography and minoring in computer science. He pursued this discipline during the day, while at night he drove a cab. Later, after getting his own car, he drove for Uber and Lyft in addition to other odd jobs he could find to pay for his schooling, a roof over his head, and other living expenses; all while saving to open his own studio.

Eighteen months after enrolling at Pasadena City College, Adam accumulated enough credits to transfer to the University of Southern

California, better known as USC. With an above-average grade point average (GPA) backed by an even more impressive portfolio, as far as his photography was concerned, Adam was awarded a full-ride scholarship. Another eighteen months later, he graduated with honors in photography while also minoring in computer science.

Photography was his life blood and computer science a hobby. He was, however, a whiz when it came to the computer. Indeed, he could venture into the dark web, meaning that he'd obtained the ability to hack into any modern electronic gadget without leaving a trace. He would do this only for fun, though. He could do wonders on the computer with the pictures that he took, and had even designed a special app to help him with that magic touch.

In no time, as his talents became known, he was contracted to photograph models, news events, landscapes, and everything else that required his Midas touch. Like many immigrants presented with a rare opportunity, Adam had developed a very strong work ethic. He had a knack for getting maximum results, even when resources were scarce. It was not long before he'd partnered with a like-minded buddy from college—also an immigrant, but from the Philippines—named Steven Basa. The two of them found an empty loft in Old Town Pasadena, turning it into a mini-studio and office where they further delved into their shared passion.

For the two young men, it was not a job, but an adventure. They worked at their craft nonstop, to a point that they were starting to get more work than they could handle. They were on the verge of a major breakthrough when the headaches came calling for Adam. At first they were not severe enough to keep him from working, and from engaging in other activities he had taken a liking to, like playing the California Super Lotto every week—just for the fun on it.

At first, he dismissed the headaches and attributed them to the strain of pushing himself to the verge of a breakdown. Being from a so-called Third World country where one did not rush to a doctor for every ailment, real or imagined, Adam continued to ignore the headaches, and as such, they got worse as the days and weeks progressed. It was at this point that his friend and business partner, Steven Basa, took it upon himself to drive him to a doctor he knew very well. And that happened to be Dr. Muhammed.

Tests were conducted, including an MRI. They waited for the results, which the doctor had promised would be ready in a few days. He prescribed some strong pain medications to help deal with the discomfort. When his patient called a day later to complain that the pills did not seem to be working, the doctor increased the dosage. That seemed to be doing the trick. However, when the hydrocodone wore off, the pain came back with a vengeance, to a point that Adam began to experience dizzy spells and blurred vision.

It was at that point Dr. Muhammed recommended that, going forward, Adam use public transportation or have a friend drive him wherever he needed to go, including to his doctor visits. He was not, under any circumstances, to get behind the wheel. What usually followed in situations like Adam's, the doctor knew—even though he had yet to share this with his patient— was that seizures were not far behind.

The tiny examination room Maria led him to after the latest bout subsided was all too familiar. It was windowless, with a small table, two chairs, and an examination bed on which he was seated. On the wall opposite the bed was a poster bearing a colored picture of the human anatomy, with all internal and external body parts labeled.

Adam Mashabela was in deep thought as he gazed at the poster with vacant eyes, wondering what pronouncements the doctor had up his sleeve when, all of a sudden, there was a soft knock at the door. Then it opened slowly.

Dr. Maurice Muhammed was a big man, six feet three inches tall, and tipped the scales at 250 pounds. He had a gray afro and deep, penetrating eyes that exuded the kindness he was known for. He still had the athletic gait of the linebacker he'd been in college, when he would steamroll over everyone and everything that stood in front of him – even life itself.

He was holding a file in his right hand, which Adam presumed contained the results of the X-ray and lab tests he had taken a few days earlier. He tried to stand up to greet the doctor, but with his free hand, the big man signaled to him that it was not necessary. The fact that the younger man always did that whenever he entered the examination room was not lost on the great physician. It reminded him, not for the first time, that his patient was a foreigner who had been well-groomed in manners.

He sighed as he forced a smile. "No, please stay seated, Adam. It's good to see you."

"Likewise, Dr. Muhammed."

The doctor was dressed in the ubiquitous white overcoat common in his profession, and a stethoscope dangling from around his neck. He placed the file on the small table at the other end of the tiny room, which now felt like a closet with the doctor present. Dr. Muhammed pulled a chair out, sat and faced his patient, who was still seated on the bed, his legs barely touching the floor.

The doctor looked his patient straight in the eye and asked, "So, how are you feeling, Adam?"

"Fine, Doctor." He paused, and then added quickly, "I mean…besides the frequent headaches, of course."

The doctor nodded and asked, "The pain medicine I prescribed for you, is it working?" His intention was to lay a cushion for the next heavy words he was about to drop on his somewhat unsuspecting patient.

"In a way, Doctor," Adam said truthfully. There was suddenly a tick, which forced him to tilt his head sideways. "They keep the pain at bay, but once they wear off, it comes back with a vengeance."

And as if on cue, the pain said 'hello'. He grimaced, leaned backwards, and rubbed his temples.

Goaded now by the pain, Adam said from between gritted teeth, "Ah! It's terrible when it comes, Doctor. The pain is brutal, and I am not sure if the pills you prescribed are strong enough. I am also starting to feel weak, dizzy, and nauseous. However, the worst part is that it is messing with my livelihood. I need steady hands to take beautiful pictures, and now even that is becoming harder and harder, because I can't hold the camera steady long enough to capture the right shot."

The doctor listened patiently, like a Catholic priest in a confession booth. The next part was going to be very difficult. He genuinely liked this young, handsome man, but what choice did he have as a doctor? This was something that had been hammered into them in medical school—not to be attached to their patients—but it was a dogma that he could not follow. He was human, after all, and not God, as some doctors tended to sometimes think they were. This was one aspect of his job he'd never fully embraced; for the news he was about to deliver could not in any way be sugar-coated or dismissed lightly.

Dr. Muhammed sighed and reached for the file he had placed earlier on the small table. In it was a manila envelope, from which he pulled out two X-rays that showed an image of a skull and a brain. He held up one of them so his patient could have a clear view of what he was about to show him.

"We managed to find out exactly what's causing these headaches, Adam," the doctor said with professional detachment as he pointed at the image of what Adam could only, and correctly so, assume was his brain.

The moment was punctuated by a long silence prior to the dreadful news both knew was coming. The doctor knew the full extent of the news, of course. However, Adam could only guess, but to what extent the patient had absolutely no idea.

"Adam, there is no nice way of saying this. Son, you have a tumor the size of a sparrow's egg. It is deep in between the cerebral lobes of your brain, so deep that nothing can be done as far as surgery or radiation is concerned. It is malignant, very deadly; what in medical terms is known as glioblastoma grade four—which, I'm afraid, is the worst kind."

Dr. Maurice 'Reese' Muhammed had, over the course of his stellar medical career, delivered awful news to his patients. It came with the territory. He had operated on cancer patients, opening them up, only to see that nothing could be done except to stitch up the unlucky soul, giving them the news that the cancer had spread and sending them home to either wait for divine intervention, or for death to claim them. The latter would occur more often than not.

He had tried in many cases to save a life, as his job required him to do, but in the end had to accept defeat. It never got any easier as the years went by to tell his patients—particularly those he had grown attached to, like this handsome young man—that they were most likely going to die, and that time would be soon.

Adam's mouth became dry in an instant as he tried to reconcile the irreconcilable.

"But I'm afraid that's not all, Adam," the doctor announced. Apparently the nightmare was not over, not by a long shot. The hits just kept coming. "The headaches, the dizziness, and the nausea will only get worse from here on out. Soon you'll begin having seizures, which will lead to complete organ failure, including your heart." All this time, those deep-set, penetrating eyes that also revealed incredible kindness never flickered or diverted from the young man for one moment. He was giving it to him straight, and not for an instant enjoying the task.

For his part, Adam listened in stunned silence; even though each word felt like a mule kick first to the stomach, and then to the groin area. He saw his entire life flash before his very eyes. This could not be happening, he thought to himself. Not now, when he had everything to live for. His career, his life, right up until the headaches became a little more than what he thought at first a temporary nuisance, was about to take off like a rocket.

Life, mother fate, he thought to himself as he digested the news, *sure has a cruel sense of humor and a keen sense of irony. She trips you up just as success is literally in the palm of your hands.*

"So, Dr. Muhammed, what does this mean? Am I going to die?" Even he was surprised at the calm voice which otherwise came in something slightly louder than a whisper.

Dr. Muhammed, totally ducking the question, said, "The important thing right now, Adam, is to stay positive."

However, his patient would not be denied. It was after all *his* life, and he had every right to know what would become of it.

"Dr. Muhammed, please tell me the truth. How long have I got to live?" Never in his twenty-four years of walking this God's green earth did Adam Mashabela ever think that his mortality had the possibility of being measured in days, months, and if lucky, a few years. The thought was overwhelming, to say the least, but as of now its gravity had yet to hit home.

"A month or two, at the most," was the doctor's gloomy answer.

The words hit like a mortar fired from less than a hundred yards away. But then again, the shock of that response had yet to register; it would only hit later.

Part of it could be that right at the moment when the doctor said that, Adam was jolted by yet another round of pain as if two hot blades were being stuck in both temples, and was thus a bit numb—or perhaps because by some strange phenomenon, the human body and psyche has a way of absorbing calamity that prevents it from going into complete meltdown. He took the news pretty well, under the circumstances.

Instead he felt tired and in some strange way relieved, now that he knew for certain that he had, at the very most, two months left to walk this earth. The news also had a sobering effect on him. He had no immediate regrets that he could think of. He was single, tied to no one. He had no siblings. Adam was primarily raised by his maternal grandmother. Both his parents had succumbed to AIDS, a disease that had continued its onslaught the world over, and especially in Africa.

Apparently his late father, Paul Mashabela, had been a philandering man who, given that he was blessed with killer good looks, found it difficult to stick with one sexual partner, and had thus contracted the deadly disease and passed it on to his wife, Neo, when Adam was still a toddler. His father had capitulated first, followed by his wife a few months later. Adam only had fleeing memories of them. Now, here was a doctor in a strange land, thousands of miles away from home, telling him that he would be joining his parents in the foreseeable future.

"But how could this have sprung up on me so fast, Doctor?" Adam wanted to know. The cold chill of frightening reality was slowly beginning to sink in.

"Unfortunately, Adam, with these types of cases, they're never easy to detect. Just like pancreatic cancer, we usually catch it when it's already too late.

Adam nodded, accepting the doctor's explanation.

"Do you have close relatives living nearby? You're going to need them."

For an answer, the handsome young man looked to the floor and shook his head. Other than his close friend and business associate Steven Basa, he was alone. The thought of going back home to Serowe and burdening his already ailing grandmother was not at all appealing.

Dr. Muhammed watched his patient as he absentmindedly opened his wallet and looked at a neatly folded piece of paper tucked at the corner among the bank notes. For a moment it looked as if he was going to pull it out, but then just as quickly thought better of it. This maneuver made the doctor wonder, albeit for a brief moment, what it was, but then he dismissed the thought. There were much more important things to prep the young man for in light of the unenviable road ahead.

"Now, Adam," the doctor continued. "I want you to know that if the pain becomes unbearable even after taking the medicine I gave you, or you feel worse in any way, don't hesitate to call me, okay? I don't care what time of day it is; just call. If it means going to the emergency room, so be it, but pick up the phone nonetheless, and I will drive you myself if need be. Is that understood?"

Adam nodded again before saying, "Yes, Dr. Muhammed, I will." At the same time, he felt a lump in his throat as he fought back tears. Not tears of self-pity, but because he was genuinely touched by the man's kindness.

He stood up to leave after the doctor wrote and handed him a prescription for a stronger dosage of the pain medicine, along with other medications to help cope with his latest lists of maladies.

The doctor then walked him to the entrance of his practice, something he very rarely did. When they reached the glass double doors, he placed his hand on the younger man's shoulder and said in a low voice, "Take care now, Adam, and remember not to give yourself anxious moments. Sometimes these things have a way of working themselves out. There is always a power greater than ourselves, greater even than medicine."

Adam stopped and turned to look at the bigger, taller man. For the first time, the doctor could see a flash of genuine sadness in the young man's eyes.

"Yes, Doctor," he agreed, and quickly added, "...but God has been too busy lately. However, he has some very serious explaining to do when I finally meet him."

The weak attempt at humor by the soon-to-be-dead young man was able to force somewhat of a chuckle from both men; and with that, Adam walked through the doors, gave the doctor one last smile and disappeared around the corner. The doctor thought of asking him if he needed a ride, but then thought better of it. Besides, he knew that his patient did not live far from his office. He guessed that Adam would walk, which might do him some good under the circumstances.

CHAPTER 3

DR. MUHAMMED STAYED ROOTED in the same spot as he watched his patient leave. He bit his lower lip in frustration and sadness as he thought of the bleak and now, almost certainly, short life ahead of the young man. For a man who never had children of his own, let alone a family, he felt as if he was losing a son. He let out a long sigh and thought to himself: *the things they never teach you at medical school.*

At last, he turned to walk back into his office, sinking onto the leather chair in the immaculately furnished room. It was semi-dark—the doctor preferred it that way whenever he felt the need to deflate, especially after delivering the news to a patient that their time was up. Looking at Adam Mashabela's file, which was placed on the shiny mahogany desk, Dr. Muhammed again wondered if he could have done more to save the young man's life. Just as after his previous ruminations, he came to the same conclusion that he had done all he could, and that at some point he would have to accept defeat. However, at the moment, that admission was far from his mind.

He then extended his arm and pressed the button on the intercom on his desk. There still was work to be done, regardless of how rotten he felt inside. This was, after all, a private practice. Patients were also customers, and he needed them to keep his doors open.

"Maria," he said into the device.

"Yes, Dr. Muhammed?" was the clear response from the other end.

"Could you come here for a moment?"

"I'll be right there," said the ever-efficient employee.

Less than a minute later, the young and pretty Hispanic lady, dressed in maroon medical scrubs common for people in her profession, was in the doctor's office. Aside from being the receptionist, Maria was also a certified nurse's aide. She had an iPad in her hand, ready to type any instructions the doctor might decide to give her. In this modern era, the electronic age, notepads and pens were slowly but surely becoming obsolete.

She looked at the doctor, who at the moment seemed spaced out to a point that she felt compelled to prompt him into the here and now. Dr. Muhammed, seated now behind his desk, had rested his feet on it, hands behind his back with his fingers dovetailed to one another and was gazing at the ceiling.

"Yes, Doctor?" she prodded for the second time, though this time it was a little louder.

As if noticing her presence for the first time, Dr. Muhammed casually took his feet off the table one at a time, and then looked at her for a brief moment. This made Maria wonder if the doctor's unusual demeanor had something to do with the cute young patient who had just left hardly fifteen minutes earlier.

"Dr. Muhammed!"

The doctor flicked his eyes, as if coming out of a trance.

"Does Adam Mashabela have any more X-rays and tests scheduled for next week?" the doctor wanted to know.

Right away, Maria worked her fingers on the iPad with amazing dexterity before looking up at the doctor.

"Not for another month," she said.

The doctor seemed to digest the answer for a moment as he grinded his molars.

"A month?"

"Yes," she responded as she wondered where the profound physician was going with this.

Dr. Muhammed then said, "You may want to cancel it. He won't be needing it." He immediately winced as he realized that he had said more than he was supposed to.

"Cancel it?" Maria raised an eyebrow, not sure she heard him correctly. "Isn't it crucial that he gets it?" Normally she would carry out her orders without question, but since she kind of had a crush on the handsome patient with the unique and exotic accent, she supposed now was the right time to make an exception.

"Like I said, he won't be needing it, Maria …
okay?"

There was something in the doctor's tone that
gave her pause. She had been surreptitiously
reading through Adam Mashabela's file, and she
knew more than she was supposed to. With that in
mind, she decided to push her luck a little.

"So what are you saying, Dr. Muhammed?"
Her eyes were suddenly wide as she
unconsciously lowered her voice. "Is Adam going
to …?"

The doctor's arm suddenly shot up like that of
a traffic cop, interrupting her before she could get
to finish her sentence.

"No, all I'm saying is *cancel* it, Maria," he
said, and for good measure added, "Is that
understood?"

It was clear now by the way he said it that that
he would not brook any further discussion into the
matter. After all, they were getting perilously
close to breaching doctor-patient privacy, and they
both knew it.

"Okay," Maria sighed. "Anything else?" She
was all business now.

Dr. Muhammed sighed, stretched his arms
and once again put his feet on the desk.

"Who's next?"

"You have Mrs. Brown in half an hour," she
announced.

The doctor consulted the chronometer on his
wrist and said, "Can you make it an hour? I need a
bit of time to reflect. I really hate giving patients

bad news." The doctor had a faraway look in his eyes, not realizing that he had slipped again.

"That bad, huh?" Maria pounced.

"Yes," the doctor answered.

"Does he have any relatives we may have to notify in case of any emergency, beside his friend Steven Basa?"

They were back in unchartered territory again, but after second thoughts the doctor saw no harm, so he gave what she wanted.

"He is a bit of a closed book when it comes to talking about himself."

"So is he all alone out here?" There was concern in her voice.

"As far as I know, yes," was the doctor's answer.

"And where is he from again?" Maria asked, knowing very well the answer to that one, but she felt the need to keep up appearances.

"Botswana." The doctor flashed a smile, the first real one of the morning. He knew that she knew, and he was also aware that she paid more attention to the young man's file than she did others.

He looked at her and smiled, which in itself revealed what he was thinking.

"What?" she smiled as she slyly avoided his gaze.

"You like him, Maria, don't you?"

"Come on, Doctor." She was blushing now as a basket hanging on the door that contained files suddenly caught her attention. She collected the files that were in it and was soon eager to get back to her station.

Changing the subject, she said just as she reached the door, "By the way, did you hear that the winning ticket was sold right here in Altadena?"

"What winning ticket?"

"For the California Super Lotto. The biggest prize ever, of four hundred and fifty-seven million dollars. Whoever bought it is the sole winner." She shook her head at the thought.

"Really? Wow! That's gonna make someone wealthy," the doctor said. In reality, he couldn't have cared less. He was just happy to talk about anything that would keep his mind off his patient.

Maria said, "Yeah, I know, right? The girls and I played like we always do." She was referring to her colleagues in the office.

"Win anything?" the doctor teased, his feet back on the desk.

Maria smiled as she reached for the doorknob and said, "Next time, maybe. And when I do, I will buy you one of those high-rise buildings in the Pasadena financial district before I move to the Bahamas."

The doctor smiled again and said, "Wouldn't that be something?"

His mind was far away, though. His thoughts were suddenly on Adam as he wondered what he was going through at that very moment.

"Yep, and you know what's sad?" Maria asked, bringing the doctor out of his reverie without knowing it. "They say the person who has the winning ticket has yet to come forward, and it's been what, three days now?"

"Maybe they don't know that they won. Anyway, let me know the moment Mrs. Brown gets here." It was a polite dismissal, and Maria took the hint.

"Will do, Doc," she said as she gently shut the door behind her.

CHAPTER 4

ADAM STEPPED OUTSIDE and into a beautiful southern California morning. Lake Avenue, which ran north and south, was not at the moment bustling with activity as it normally was. This part of town, the northern side of Altadena, was the quiet part. Diagonally opposite Dr. Muhammed's practice was a popular hangout known as the *Coffee Gallery*. It was here that up-and-coming artists, bands, and standup comedians plied their trade; including those who needed a caffeine rush.

It was to this place that Adam's feet took him. Normally he would have called an Uber to take him home, which was a few blocks up the street, or he could have easily walked and been at his apartment in less than half an hour if he so wished, but today he lacked the strength. He was in a trance—dazed, confused, but most of all frightened as he strutted along the sidewalk like a newborn fawn, his mind in turmoil as the doctor's voice echoed in his ears. "*Six weeks, Adam ... six weeks ... six weeks ... the tumor, a grade four glioblastoma ... six weeks ... six weeks ..."*

He sighed as reality slowly started weighing in. He, Adam Mashabela, a young foreigner who had beaten the odds and migrated all alone, facing a far from certain future, had been able to cultivate a niche for himself. He'd chased a dream that was illusive at first, but again, against all odds, he was beginning to settle into a life that even he had never dreamt possible—compounded by the fact that just three days earlier, a great consecration had befallen him out of nowhere—only to have *everything* crumble because of a brain tumor.

He, Adam Mashabela, was going to be dead in a matter of weeks. Dead in a foreign land. Far from his motherland, his people, his ancestors, and his dear old beloved grandmother. Just the thought of calling and letting her know that this was the end, was at the moment far removed from the realms of reality. The feeling alone was devastating.

Somehow the prospect of dying did not scare him; he was beginning to accept it. What made him shudder as he crossed the street toward the Coffee Gallery, via a designated pedestrian crossing area, was the aftermath. What waited for him on the other side? Was where he was headed cold, dark, lonely, and scary, as it had always been in his nightmares? Or was the place that awaited him even scarier than his imagination would allow? Would he be counting millenniums instead of years in a place with no doors?

Adam felt giddy. His head was in turmoil, and with it finally came the grief. He spotted a bus bench he had hardly noticed in the past. It was situated right on the sidewalk in front of the barbershop next door to the Gallery. He sank onto it without giving the process much thought. His legs were weak anyway, and could not carry him any further as he placed his elbows on his knees, face in his palms, and without a care in the world began to weep openly.

Meanwhile, inside the Coffee Gallery, a tall blond bombshell named Lucy Young was paying for her mango smoothie. She smiled at the cashier as he handed her the change, revealing a perfect set of teeth and a pair of dimples that punctuated both cheeks. The Coffee Gallery was almost always frequented by beautiful women who came in all shapes, sizes, and races, but Lucy Young was the kind of beauty who could stop traffic without really trying, and today was no exception.

Having moved to Altadena a little over three months ago from Laguna Beach, Lucy was relatively new to the area. A recent graduate in chiropractic medicine, she had found employment with a private practitioner also on Lake Avenue. The office was at a plaza located three blocks north of the Gallery and Dr. Muhammed's office. She had a half-day today and was on her way to the gym. Even though she was dressed in a skirt that crawled a little above her knees to reveal shapely legs, along with pumps and a matching blouse, the woman was still stunning.

She took a sip from her plastic cup as she stepped out of the store. She turned right, which meant she was heading south on Lake. Her car, a late-model, light blue convertible Mini Cooper, was parked on the side street. The past couple of weeks had been busy at the office, forcing her to clock in long hours even after the regular day had ended, which was why she was looking forward to her time at the gym this early sunny afternoon. A five-mile run on the treadmill and a few calisthenics would be enough to take the edge off and relieve her of the stress that had bogged her down lately.

As Lucy smiled to herself in anticipation of the day ahead, she was confronted by a strange sight that froze her dead in her tracks. She looked left, and then right; the sidewalk was empty, but that was not what froze her. A man, a young black man at that, was seated alone on a bus bench a few feet away. Nothing unusual about that, except that he was hunched over, weeping openly as if he had lost a loved one. His shoulders heaved up and down, sideways and then backwards, as one heart-wrenching wail was followed by another. It was painful to watch.

Lucy Young, an only child, was raised by God-fearing liberal parents; she was from an upper-middle-class background with parents who were fiercely devoted to one another. They attended church regularly, tithed every Sunday because the bible said so, paid their taxes because that's what the law required; but what was more important was that Mr. and Mrs. Young preached and practiced high moral values.

She was born and raised in Laguna Beach, California, a seaside resort city located in southern Orange County, and also one of the most beautiful cities in southern California that attracted tourists from all over the globe by the droves, especially during the summer months. The exclusive beach city is known for its mild year-round climate, scenic coves, environmental preservation, and a thriving artist community. Her parents were semi-retired and had been very successful in their respective careers; meaning that Lucy's upbringing was privileged and pretty much sheltered. However, if there one thing her parents had instilled in her, it was the belief in being kind to those less fortunate—and the United States, not to mention the entire world over, had many such people.

Attending a college outside Laguna Beach later in life opened her eyes to the reality of the plight suffered by many of her nation's people. Her friends at school would laugh at her, call her clueless and naïve whenever she would strike up a conversation with the so-called 'bums', homeless men and women who were scattered all over southern California like weeds. People she would sometimes give loose change, and every so often buy them something to eat. She also at times, when her schedule permitted, would volunteer a few hours at a local homeless shelter for women and children in Pasadena known as *Door Of Hope*.

Thus, when she saw the young man seated on the bench bawling his eyes out, her first instinct was to find out what the problem was—but sometimes that could be a mistake. Even though Altadena was a relatively safe city backed by a sheriff's department that was said to be ranked among the best in the nation, it was sometimes a good idea to mind your own business; lest you get accosted by some young black punk who for all she knew could be crying over a girlfriend leaving him, or worse, a court order by a judge who had just ordered him to surrender himself to the authorities and head to jail. It happened all the time. Besides, she had a date with the 24 Hour Fitness Gym located further south in downtown Pasadena, and this was an appointment she had no intention of missing.

These were the thoughts going through the beautiful Lucy Young's mind as she pulled her car keys from her Kate Spade handbag, passing the weeping stranger from behind without so much as a glance. She was just about to press the button on her keypad to deactivate the alarm on her vehicle when she stopped and backtracked. Her conscience and curiosity had gotten the best of her.

Adam's eyes were tightly shut as he hunched over, his sobs slowly subsiding to sniffles. It had all happened when he practically fell on the bench and the floodgate of tears opened. Still, the first indication he had that someone was now standing beside him was the fragrance, a sweet-smelling and yet intoxicating perfume that made him open his eyes, sit up, and stare into the most striking face he had ever seen; so much such that he almost gasped.

Looking up at her, Adam could tell that the beautiful white woman who looked to be in her early to mid-twenties like him was tall, perhaps five feet seven or so, and built like a supermodel with high cheekbones, a perfect mouth, and a nose that revealed a Scandinavian ancestry. Nevertheless, what drew him in were her deep green eyes that glistened like bright emeralds. The eyes were penetrating in an almost sensual and magical way, and for a moment the young man from Serowe had to wonder if this was an apparition, part of his tumor playing tricks, because no creation could be that beautiful—at least, that's what he told himself.

In his life, Adam Mashabela had seen many beautiful women back home, and later in California, which was the melting pot for all nationalities far and wide. In his profession as a professional photographer, he had learned to notice even the minutest of details normally missed by the ordinary eye, be it a human being, animal, picture, sculpture, or landscape. Basically anything or anyone he would deem necessary to have him pick up one of his numerous cameras, depending on the mood he wished to convey, and snap a few shots. But this goddess, who had appeared seemingly out of nowhere, topped them all.

33

Her white skin was smooth, free of any blemish, as if nature herself had picked up her delicate brush and wiped away any specks. She had a bit of a tan, and a face that looked as though it would break into a dazzling smile any minute. However, that beautiful face was, at the moment at least, slightly contorted in a way that reflected genuine concern.

Her perfectly lined lips parted to say, "Excuse me, sir, are you all right?" Even the trumpets of the archangels in the high heavens would have never done justice to describe what, to Adam Mashabela's ears, was a melodious tune!

He looked up at her, not bothering to wipe his tears, stunned to a point that words failed him. Words that would have sounded something like, *'Oh nothing, miss, I just got the worse news imaginable from my doctor that I have an inoperable brain tumor, and according to his expert prognosis, I will be dead in six weeks, how about that?'* Yet at the moment, none of that mattered—the tumor and the subsequent death sentence, and the other news he'd gotten the night before the doctor's visit that he could hardly process, because he was hit by one nauseating pain after another. Right now his soul, every fiber of his being, was laser-focused on the beauty standing barely three feet away from him.

When he did not answer her, she asked again, pulling a smartphone out of her bag. "Sir, are you all right? Would you like me to call someone?"

Feeling a bit foolish, Adam quickly used the back of his hand to wipe his tears, and then

34

frantically searched his pockets for a tissue or handkerchief. The beautiful woman noticed this and quickly handed him a napkin she had gotten with her smoothie.

"Oh, thanks," he sniffed and then quickly added, "N-no, I am fine, ma'am."

She noticed a trace of an accent she could not place right away, and the fact that he had addressed her as 'ma'am' was not lost on her. Definitely a foreigner, and raised right, based on what she could deduce from their brief exchange so far. But she was not buying his response.

"Come on, something is definitely wrong," she pressed on. "Can I get you something? Or call someone?"

He sat up straight and tried very hard to appear normal, but the tears kept flowing nonetheless, and at the moment he could not stop them. His big eyes were red now from the prolonged weeping, and Lucy's heart melted in sympathy. For some strange reason, she felt drawn to the handsome young stranger. Thoughts of hitting the gym evaporated as soon as she decided to try and get to the bottom of whatever it was that was troubling this man.

"No, ma'am, really. I'm fine, it's just … it's just that I received some not-so-good news, if you know what I mean." Adam immediately grimaced as he realized that he had said more than he intended to. No one, much less this pretty woman, would have to know that he was not long for this world.

"Someone died?" she wanted to know. In Lucy's mind, that was the most logical explanation as to why someone would weep so openly – especially if that someone was a man.

Men, especially young men, were good at hiding their feelings. Though now that she was confronted by this sad sight, there was something attractive about it. Real men—strong, tough men, she believed—were never afraid of displaying their feminine side. This surely was a first.

"Nothing of the sort," Adam said. *The only person who will soon be dead is me,* he thought but did not say. "It's ... I ... I'd rather not talk about it."

Lucy decided to press on nonetheless. "Your girlfriend left you?" she asked, not trying to be funny or sound teasing. Why else would a guy cry so openly in public, if losing a loved one was not to blame? But even as she said that, she wondered what kind of foolish girl would leave a good-looking guy like this one.

Adam looked away before giving an answer. In that brief moment when their gaze had met, Lucy could tell that there was a faraway look in his eyes.

"Oh, no. I haven't had time to think about women, to be quite honest."

It was true. He was so focused on his career that the few relationships he'd had in the past, mostly at college, were few and far between. Still, even he had to wonder why he was revealing so much about himself to a total stranger. Normally he would clam up, thank the lady for her concern, tell her he was all right and be on his way to forestall any further conversation—but not today. He had to wonder again if it was the tumor doing the talking for him.

Lucy, on the other hand, found his childlike honesty to be quite refreshing and genuinely satisfying, which piqued her curiosity even more—and her attraction, she reluctantly admitted to herself. The two stared at one another for an awkward moment, Adam lost again in those enchanting green eyes. Was it possible that a woman could be that pretty without any immediate or discernable flaw?

She broke the brief spell by saying, "The Coffee Gallery is still open. Can I get you something—water, coffee, or a soda maybe? My name is Lucille Young, by the way, but you can call me Lucy. And you are?"

She smiled, revealing that perfect set of white, sparkling teeth and cheeks dotted by dimples. Her smile was dazzling as it was inebriating.

Jesus H. Christ, Adam thought to himself, *what a beauty!* He in turn extended his arm to meet her slender and delicate one for a handshake. The touch itself was sensual, almost erotic.

"Adam, Adam Mashabela. Pleased to meet you, Lucy, and hey, sorry for all this. Just something I have to deal with." Again he caught himself revealing too much, but he didn't care anymore. Callous as it sounded, he would be dead in six weeks, so why care? By now the tears were long gone.

"Mashabela," she said with a smile, intrigued by the unusual last name. He, on the other hand, liked the way the name rolled off her tongue. "And it's not a problem at all, Adam Mashabela," she smiled again. "It's not every day that you see a man crying in public."

Adam was slightly embarrassed as he forced a smile. He looked away—tearing his gaze away was more like it—just so he would not get lost in those bewitching green eyes yet again.

When she realized that she had somewhat hit a nerve, she quickly changed the subject, her curiosity piqued once again as she brushed a strand of blonde hair from her forehead.

"Do I notice an accent?"

In truth, Adam had been trying to lose his accent ever since he immigrated to the United States. But it was still there, all the same.

"Yes indeed." He was now quickly recovering from his grief, and this beauty standing before him was the antidote – no doubt.

"Let me guess. The Islands, Jamaica maybe?" She smiled as she touched her lower lip with a long, polished and well-manicured forefinger. My God, she was gorgeous, and Adam felt as if he had been hit by a thunderbolt.

"No, southern Africa. Botswana, to be exact."

"Figures."

He was taken aback by her response.

"Excuse me?" he asked, genuinely surprised.

"I knew you could not be American," she chuckled ever so slightly.

"And why's that?" Adam wanted to know, intrigued to say the least.

"For the most part, American men don't like showing their emotions in public—if they can help it, that is. It's part of that macho culture they think is cool, if you ask me. So that's why I got curious. It's heartwarming and says a lot about a man who is not afraid to cry, especially out in the open."

He gave her a look that seemed to say *'You Americans are surely a bunch of strange people.'*

Aloud he said, "You seem to know a lot about this kind of thing, Lucy, don't you?"

He was enjoying this exchange immensely. The two had hit it off without giving any of it a second thought. They looked and sounded like two old college buddies catching up on some old gossip.

"Psych was my minor in college," she said as she shifted her weight from one foot to the other.

"Psychology?"

"Yes." She flashed that enchanting smile yet again.

"And what was your major?" Adam wanted to know, totally intrigued and not making conversation just for the sake of making it, but truly wanting to know more about this woman—as she obviously, by the looks of it, wanted the same out of him.

She looked around and said, "Are you sure you want to talk about all that out here? The sun is pretty strong today. I got a better idea—why don't we go inside, I'll get you that cup of coffee if you're not in a hurry, and I can tell you all about

it. Is that okay, Adam? That's the least I can do."
Lucy was inwardly pleased with herself that she
had, for the moment at least, diverted Adam's
attention from whatever malady he was facing and
onto something more pleasant.

Adam, on the other hand, could not believe
his luck. One minute he was grief-stricken, finally
horrified by the fact that he would be dead in less
than two months, when there was so much to live
for—in other words, the worst news anyone could
ever get. And then out of nowhere a beauty walks
into his life, striking up a conversation with him in
a way that made him forget about everything –
especially his mortality.

"Wouldn't hurt, I suppose. Thanks, Lucy," he
said as if this kind of thing happened to him every
day.

He got up slowly. Adam had long ago learned
that if he stood up quickly, pain shot up from his
back right to his temples, causing instant dizziness
and nausea. Now he knew why.

CHAPTER 5

SINCE IT WAS A LITTLE AFTER MIDDAY, and a weekday at that, the Coffee Gallery was virtually empty. So Adam and Lucy were able to find a table for two in the back corner of the room, where they could talk without being disturbed. The more they were in each other's presence, the clearer it became that a mutual attraction between the two was brewing. Following Lucy's recommendation, Adam also got a mango smoothie.

He took a sip through a straw and smacked his lips. It was so refreshingly delicious. Lucy watched him with a smile planted on her face. For some strange reason, even though she had barely met this man, she felt comfortable in his presence. There was a welcoming aura about him that she could not explain.

"So, photography is your thing?" she asked as she leaned forward, arms on the table in front of her. It was obvious that she was intrigued by his career choice.

"My life," Adam said proudly, the tumor forgotten for now. "I'm normally at peace when I have a camera in my hands." He went on to name the different brands of cameras that he owned.

"Why don't you have one of them with you now?" The woman was way too observant, he quickly noticed. "Because I read somewhere that professional photographers never leave home without a camera."

True, he thought, and wondered how on earth she knew that. He paused ever so slightly, embarrassed. In truth, he did not have his camera because he had a doctor's appointment, a topic he knew if broached would create questions he was not ready to answer—not now, and maybe not ever. So he did what every person does when cornered. He deflected.

"Oh, I had a personal matter I needed to attend to that required me not to have a camera in my possession. Did I mention I am a computer whiz too?" Normally modesty was his trait, especially when dealing with someone he'd just met, but he thought since he had not much time left, what would be the harm of blowing his own trumpet?

Conversely, Lucy had to wonder what that 'personal matter' was all about, and if it had anything to do with what she saw earlier when she laid eyes on him for the first time. She instantly discarded the thought. It was none of her business, and besides it would be rude to pry any more than she already had.

"So, what kind of pictures interest you? What I really want to know is where your inspiration comes from."

Adam smiled long and hard. This was a first, and he had not smiled for a while. Lucy returned the smile as she lifted her arm and rested her chin on her palm, one elbow on the table.

"Oh, he's smiling at last," she teased. "I must have hit a nerve."

He blushed and smiled yet again, feeling more alive than he cared to remember, all because of the tall bolt of lightning from out of the blue seated a few feet away from him.

"My inspiration," Adam said with the look of someone well-versed in a subject he was about to broach, "comes from anything and everything, Lucy. It could be an old magazine, a childhood memory, anything." He paused for a brief moment and looked at her before adding, "Or even a beautiful woman."

This time it was Lucy Young who was blushing. It did not take a rocket scientist to guess that the last comment was meant for her.

"I've also been intrigued by life, and the afterlife."

"The afterlife?" she wondered aloud as she sat up straight. "Really?"

"Sometimes," he said, immediately realizing that he may have opened yet another can of worms.

"Is there a lot of belief in the afterlife where you come from? Botswana, right?"

"Right."

"Lovely, and you got your degree from?"

"The University of Southern California. Working on my master's, as a matter of fact," he said proudly.

"USC?" Lucy's eyes were wide open. There could only be one USC.

"Yes … why?" Adam asked, his antennae suddenly up.

"I went there too. Wow, a fellow Trojan. Who would have thought?"

Located in south central Los Angeles, the roughest neighborhood in the city save for Watts, the University of Southern California is paradoxically a private institution of higher learning that attracts mostly students who not only have above-average academic standing, but are also from wealthy families from around the country – even the far-off farmlands of North and South Dakota. The school also has a great scholarship program that allows deserving students, like the one Adam Mashabela once was, but on the whole had a very high Caucasian populace in its student demographic—which was why, really, it could not have come as a complete surprise that Lucy was an alumni of the university.

What remained unspoken, but came as a relief, nevertheless, was that neither of them had attended the dreaded and also hated UCLA, the University of California at Los Angeles, since the schools were bitter rivals and had been from time immemorial. The contention of these two schools ran deep, especially when it came to sports.

"Are you serious?" Adam asked, genuinely pleased and surprised.

"Yeah, class of 2010," Lucy said.

"This has got to be fate," Adam said. "I was class of 2008."

Lucy smiled, and then added, "The year Barack Obama won the election to be president of the United States." She wanted to add that she had campaigned for the man, but right now was not the time to bring up politics, a whole different animal.

"Yes, I know," Adam smiled.

It also meant at some point, their academic lives had intersected. They were at USC at the same time but never knew of each other's existence then, because they obviously ran in different circles, only to meet under somewhat bizarre circumstances in a city far from their homes—and in Adam's case much, much further away.

Time just flew by, and neither of them noticed. That was until Lucy looked at the clock on the screen of her smartphone. She had planned to meet a friend after going to the gym, and to return a few phone calls on her landline when she got home. Suddenly it was time for her to leave. She didn't want to but she knew she had to; her plans for the gym had long been abandoned.

She reached out and touched his hand ever so gently. "Look, Adam, we should do this again." She stood up, shouldering her designer bag. "I almost forgot that I have to meet a girlfriend. I'm already half an hour late, because I was having such a great time." She smiled again. That enchanting beam, which she iced with a wink. He felt he could just sit there and stare at her all day and night and not get tired. She had the look that some African poet said '*gave the eye a feast*'.

Was this infatuation, he wondered, or was everything about this beauty perfect? He deliberated again as he gritted his teeth. The pain was returning, and this time with a vengeance, but again he managed to fight it off.

She must have noticed, because that beautiful smile suddenly vanished, replaced by a look of concern.

"Are you all right?"

"I'm fine, Lucy," he said quickly as he stood to shake her hand. "Don't let me hold you."

They shook hands and smiled. Their eyes met again, and there was no denying the fact that they liked one another. It was the classic case of love at first sight.

He continued by saying, "It was a great pleasure meeting you, Lucy, and thanks for everything. You brightened up my day."

"Oh, that's so sweet, Adam, and you're very welcome."

Their hands stayed intertwined for a few seconds longer as they silently stared into each other's eyes. The silence between them spoke volumes, and it was loud. There was absolutely no doubt about it as the sparks flew between them. They were attracted to one another, and the spell was broken after they finally let go, and Adam sat down.

At that moment he remembered something, so he took out his wallet from his front pocket and pulled out a business card that he handed to her.

"Here you go, Lucy, take it. That's my business card. It has information on my website, and on it you can view my work, basically a collection of some of the best pictures I have taken over the years."

What he did not mention, even though the intention was clear to both of them, was that he was really giving her his phone number and hoping that she would reciprocate.

"Thanks, Adam, I bet they must be great. I can't wait." And she really meant it.

"Don't raise your hopes," he said, fighting the urge not to massage his temples. It was time to pop another Oxycontin.

"Come on, Adam." She smiled, revealing those sexy dimples again. "You freelance for the *Los Angeles Times,* the *LA Weekly*, and the *Pasadena Star News,* among others," she continued. "How many people get to say that?"

It was clear that a lot had been said during the time they were seated at the table earlier as one topic rolled to another with remarkable ease, just two old friends talking and catching up on old gossip. At least, that's the image they portrayed to anyone who saw them.

As an afterthought, just as she was turning to leave, she said "Oh, I almost forgot. Here's my number, you ready? I'll text it to you," she said, looking at his card, the other hand on the phone ready to text.

"Great," Adam grinned. In his mind, it was mission accomplished.

"That's your cell, right?" she asked as she took a closer look at the card between her thumb and forefinger.

"Yes."

She then heaved a deep sigh and patted him gently on the shoulder. The touch itself sent a jolt of sparks through his body that in some strange way momentarily calmed the pain.

"Look, I know we just met, Adam, but if you feel down again, please don't hesitate to call—that is, if you feel like talking."

He gave yet another toothy grin. "You're too kind, Lucy." He was doing backflips in his head.

How often did a beautiful woman who cared for the wellbeing of a stranger fall onto his lap the way this one did? Surely they had better things to do than to go out of their way to do what this woman just did for him.

"Take care. Are you sure you don't need a ride, or anything else?" she asked at least for the fifth time.

"Not at all, Lucy, you've done more than enough already. Plus I live close by." He almost suggested something stupid like *please feel free to stop by, I could surely appreciate the company of a comely female these last few days I have on God's beautiful green earth*, but he wisely bit his tongue instead. He had imposed too much on this woman already.

However, it occurred to him that thoughts and emotions he was not accustomed to were assailing him over and above. He wondered again if it was not because of the diagnosis – the death sentence, really – he was given.

"See you around," she said as she at last turned to leave.

He watched her go, and followed her with his gaze until she disappeared through the entrance of the establishment, and smiled again before he was visited by yet another wave of pain, followed by nausea. He practically ran to the bathroom as he massaged his temples, and a few minutes later he was bent over the porcelain toilet bowl, puking his guts out. On the other hand, the image of a smiling Lucy helped him through this discomfort, and for the hundredth time since he first laid eyes on her, he wished he had his camera.

CHAPTER 6

ADAM MASHABELA LOVED COMING HOME. His apartment, a bungalow really, was one of six in a large compound. The two-bedroom identical units were not connected to each other, which gave the tenants a sense of privacy and home ownership. Located on Mendocino Street off Lake Avenue at the north part of Altadena, it gave the residents in the area a marvelous view of the Mount Wilson foothill range.

A few amenities were all within walking distance. There was a Chase Manhattan Bank, a Bank of America, a United States Post Office on Lake, a few restaurants, an Aldi's supermarket. And coincidentally, Lake Plaza, where Lucy's office was located, was less than two blocks down Lake Avenue heading south, where it intersected with Calaveras Street.

The walk from the Coffee Gallery to his apartment did him a world of good. It was a struggle at first, as his legs felt weak. Lake Avenue runs north to south, stretching all the way from the outskirts of San Marino in the south up to where it ends at the foothills of Mount Wilson, which meant Adam was walking uphill. Normally, given the devastating news he'd received from Dr. Muhammed, he should have been despondent. But his chance encounter with the beautiful woman changed what for all intents and purposes should have been the most terrible day of his life.

As he walked up the now-busy street, his legs getting stronger with every stride and finally getting the blood flowing, the image of a smiling Lucy became all the more clear in his mind's eye. He replayed their conversation over and over as he smiled to himself. The idea let alone the fear, that his mortality was now in serious doubt was long forgotten.

He was a man clearly hit by a thunderbolt; there was absolutely no denying that. Adam quickened his pace as his apartment building came into view. He had made a left turn on his street, Mendocino, and the premises that housed his dwelling was half a block down the street on the left where the street ended at the intersection with El Molino Street, which ran parallel with Lake Avenue. It was a quiet middle-class neighborhood.

Adam made another left turn onto the paved driveway of his premises. His apartment was the third one among the six. As he unlocked the door, he thought again about what he was about to do. He rationalized the act by saying to himself that he was not long for this world, and that he was hurting no one.

For a bachelor, his apartment was well-furnished and nicely kept. His maid, a young

Hispanic woman named Rosalinda, came in three times a week. The living room walls had framed pictures and mementos of his craft. Since he lived alone in a two-bedroom apartment, the extra room was where he kept his cameras, other equipment related to his trade, and most important of all, his high-powered computer, set up with two flat screens next to each other on a huge mahogany desk. The room was constantly dark by choice, because sometimes he processed negatives of the pictures he took in here. No one, not even Rosalinda, was allowed access into the room. Even when alone in his apartment, as he always was, he would lock himself inside.

Today he went straight for the room, and as always locked himself in. After waiting for his eyes to get accustomed to the dark, he sat at his desk and turned on the computer and other gadgets under the desk, and waited for the screens to light up. He worked his fingers on the keyboard, and as he waited for the prompts to appear on the screen, he took out two Oxycontins from his pocket and swallowed them down with a glass of water he always kept in the room. It took a moment for the pills to dull the pain before he pulled out a pair of headphones from the side of his desk and covered his ears.

Soon thereafter, following the necessary passwords that led him from one screen to another, he at last punched in a number he had since committed to memory in the blank space—a phone number, it turned out, because he could immediately hear two distinct female voices. That of Lucy, and another he soon learned was Emily. He had successfully hacked into her network's server mainframe, and thus could listen to her calls without her ever knowing. Her provider wouldn't know either, because he made certain that the signal, if traced, could not lead back to him. It bounced all around the world, making it virtually impossible for someone to track him.

Adam knew full well the ramifications of what he was doing. No system was foolproof. Even though he was a self-taught hacker who'd written a program that fundamentally could not be traced to him, there was always that possibility of capture. What he was doing was an egregious violation of many cyber laws, almost all of them felonies that could have him locked up for a very long time.

But then again, the fact that he would soon be dead gave him the justification in his mind that he might as well have some fun before the end. Besides, seeing, meeting, and talking to that woman earlier in the day gave him a euphoric feeling that nothing in his life could come close to matching. Being in her presence, her feel, her touch, the smell of her expensive perfume made him feel alive – and so would hearing her voice.

He had caught their conversation almost right at the beginning, and he had guessed correctly that Lucy would be on her phone and talking the moment she reached her destination, or right before.

Lucy: Hey, Emily, it's me. Sorry I'm running late, but I should be there in less than twenty.

Emily: Yeah, I've been wondering what happened to you.

Lucy: Oh, I ran into this gorgeous guy.

Adam leaned closer with a smile on his face. This was good. Some distance away, the friend, faceless in his mind, let out a squeal of delight.

Emily: Do tell, I like that.

Lucy: He was crying.

Emily: (In mock amazement) No! A mama's boy?

Lucy: (Chuckles) Nothing of the sort. This one's different, and he's a foreigner. You should hear his accent. Made my knees so weak that I almost tore off my panties.

At that moment, on hearing that last statement, a jolt of electricity ran through Adam's body and he had to stifle a scream of joy, even though there was zero chance of the two women suspecting that someone else out there was listening to their conversation. This was *really* good. This was heaven.

Emily: I can see why he's different. He's foreign.

Lucy: No, it's not that. There's a side of him, a kind of mysterious dark side. Not dark as in bad, but the type you want to get to know, and did I mention that he's black?

Emily: (chuckling) I kind of had an inkling that you were gonna tell me he is, but that doesn't matter, does it?

Lucy: No, not at all. I will tell you more when I get there, but girlfriend, what a babe!

Emily: Yeah, the joy of being single, right? Because you get to sample all the time.

Lucy: It's really not that at all, Emily. This one just fell from the sky and onto my lap. You know what I mean, girl? You can call it fascination, but it was really nothing like that. I fell for him the moment his big eyes stared right at me, and like I said, I'll tell you more when I get there. I gotta hang up now, I'm driving, I'll be there in a few. Ciao.

The connection went dead, and on Adam's screen the erratic up-and-down line that indicated there was conversation on the other end suddenly became straight, and then slowly faded to black. He smiled to himself again in the darkness as he methodically removed his headphones and placed them on the desk. He was not the least bit perturbed that he was being intrusive. In fact, he was pleased with himself as he swiveled his chair and pondered in the dark. Lucy could have waited until she got to her friend's house and had this conversation in person, but she didn't. In his inflamed imagination, she was just as excited and in love as he was.

"She's mine," he muttered to himself.

He wondered, though, how she would react if she knew about his condition, and the big secret he had that came in the form of a piece of paper currently tucked away in a secret compartment of his wallet.

And just as quickly as the thought came to his mind, he took out the leather wallet, removed the piece of paper and placed it under some folded papers in the bottom drawer, and then locked it. There was no sense in carrying it around, knowing what he would do with it. Life surely had a cruel sense of humor, he thought to himself again, and then he decided at that very moment that he was going to live it to the fullest—*every* minute of it.

Lucille 'Lucy' Yvette Young, a woman he had met barely two hours ago, had given him purpose. The sight of her gave him life, and he was going to do everything in his power from that moment on to make certain that he saw her, even from a distance, without her being aware of it. To him, she was now the source of his life. She *was* his life, he decided.

He stood up and, still in the dark, walked across the room and pulled a shiny silver case from where he always kept it. He knelt down, dialed the necessary combination and opened it. Inside was a velvet casing with various components that held his favorite camera, and the Zeiss lenses that came with it. From them he picked the best, screwed it on, and turned the digital camera on. On the viewfinder, he checked to see if all was in order, and after making certain that it was, he made all the necessary adjustments to make certain that it could capture images in the dark. When all was good and ready, camera still in hand, he at last turned on the light.

CHAPTER 7

THE NEIGHBORHOOD IN PASADENA at the south side of the 210 freeway and the famous Colorado Boulevard, which ran east to west cutting through the city, had beautiful homes, condominiums, and apartments for the simple reason that it was occupied mostly by the well-to-do who lived in that part of the city. Furthermore, it was in this area where the floats of the annual Rose Parade, on the first day of the New Year, could be seen up close and personal by those lucky and brave enough to camp overnight (as this happens during the height of winter), along the streets where the floats passed in order to get a great view.

Further west on Colorado Boulevard is the famed 'Old Town Pasadena.' An area as old as the city itself, well preserved but always bustling with activity, particularly in the summer months. A little further west, Colorado Boulevard intersects with Orange Grove Boulevard, a street lined with palm trees like almost any other in the city. Further south on the street, the neighborhood is more pristine, and among the homes is a beautiful apartment building that looked like a cottage on the beautiful countryside of the Swiss Alps.

This is an affluent neighborhood of the city, made famous by the fact that the Rose Parade assembles at this area before it sets out on its thirteen-mile run. This is where Lucy Yvette Young's apartment was located, a two-bedroom she called home that faced Orange Grove Boulevard. The duplex in which her apartment was had a paved driveway that cut through the compound.

The property was surrounded by nicely manicured hedges, a lawn, and two palm trees on either side of the driveway. It was already twilight when Lucy's Mini Cooper pulled into the driveway and parked at her assigned space. It had been three days since she met Adam, and there had thus far been no communication between the two. The typical game young people play of not sounding too eager to contact the other after the initial meeting and let a few days pass; especially if both parties knew at their first meeting that there had been an obvious attraction between them.

She stepped out of the car the moment the ignition was turned off. Lucy had a phone to her ear, talking incessantly to someone. Those who knew Lucy, and knew her well, would swear laughingly that sometimes it looked as if the device was surgically attached to the left side of her head. She opened the back and took out two grocery bags from a nearby Ralphs Supermarket. One of the bags contained perishables, and the other had cleaning supplies.

Lucy was still talking on the phone when she realized that it would be difficult to carry the bags and talk on the phone at the same time.

"Hold on, I just got home," she said to whoever it was she was talking to.

She was dressed in a nice blue skirt, a tight pink blouse, and flat shoes. After placing the bags on the floor by her feet, she unlocked the door and was soon in her living room. Like Adam, Lucy lived alone, which meant she earned a pretty penny from her job—particularly when one noted how beautifully furnished her home was. The place was nice and cozy, and after placing the goods on the kitchen table, she walked back to the living room and checked to see if she had any messages on her landline. The machine indicated that she had none. Darkness was setting in very fast, it seemed, because she turned on the lights and then headed back to the kitchen to pick up her smartphone, which she had left on the table next to her grocery bags, and again spoke into it.

"Sorry, I'm gonna have to call you back, Stephanie. My hands are full."

She thereafter placed the phone on the table and started putting the food away. Lucy was a health nut, apparently, because most of the food, even the meat, was organic. The perishables were placed in the fridge, and the other stuff like fruits and bread she put in their designated places. She then left the kitchen and headed to the bedroom.

Her bedroom was just as cozy, and by all accounts indicated that she was a single woman. There was a framed picture by her bedside table that showed a much younger Lucy flanked by both parents, all of them smiling, the hair of the two women fluttering in the wind with an ocean in the background. A happy moment frozen in time.

She went into her bathroom after undressing and began brushing her teeth. Soon thereafter, she was enjoying a nice hot shower, indicated by the fact that she was humming a soft tune to herself over and over as she applied the conditioner and shampoo to her shoulder-length hair. Through the frosted glass of the shower, she looked like a Greek goddess.

A little later, she was dressed in a Victoria's Secret gown, seated on her couch in the living room. Her hair was wrapped in a towel as she paged through the latest 'Fashion' magazine. The television was on, but she hardly paid any attention to it. There was a cup in her left hand, and from it she was sipping at some hot cocoa.

One thing her living room had was a large window, meaning that someone from outside could see her clearly, if they so wished.

⌒⌒⌒⌒

Someone was watching her. And that someone had been doing so for the past three days, and that someone was doing a pretty good job of staying hidden in the shadows, and everywhere else. For the past three days, he had been stalking her like a nemesis. He followed her to her place of work, her gym, her visits to a few of her female friends, when she went to the grocery store, and had even followed her home on several occasions.

Each time, whenever he could and always from a vantage point, Adam Mashabela would snap pictures of her with his state-of-the-art camera.

Tonight his camera was fitted with a high-power telephoto zoom lens that under the circumstances, considering that it was dark, was doing a fine job at capturing her. With the towel wrapped around her head, she looked oh, so beautiful! This was compounded by the fact that Adam was high and in a state of euphoria, thanks in no small part to the shot of morphine he took before engaging on this undertaking. Crouched behind a bush of flowers and dressed in black pants, a black hoodie, and black sneakers, Adam was pretty much well hidden. He was by now well versed with the other tenants who lived on the premises, and knew their comings and goings. Other than occasionally going out to dump the trash or walk their dog, they pretty much kept indoors at this time of day.

Tonight he decided to be a bit more daring. Again feeling more alive at the sight of her, a phenomenon that never failed, he moved ever so closer to her living room window—this after making certain that no one was watching. He knew full well what would happen if someone saw him lurking around, but as one might expect, it was easy to push that troubling thought out of his mind by thinking of the six weeks he was told were all he had left.

He adjusted the lens on his camera, making sure that he had the correct reading of as much light he could get, and clicked away in rapid succession. Inside the living room, Lucy absentmindedly paged through the magazine, absolutely unaware that a pair of eyes was watching her with the zeal of a hawk. She soon sighed and yawned, obviously bored out of her mind as she reached for the remote, pointed it at the plasma TV screen and flipped through the channels. She paused momentarily, as a newscaster was saying something that caught her attention. Listening with half an ear, the anchor woman was saying:

"It's been over five days now, and still the sole winner of the $457 million California lottery has yet to come forward. There is speculation that whoever it is may have the winning ticket and does not know it ..."

Lucy sighed and muttered to herself, "Oooolala, you lucky someone. Think of what you could do with $457 million."

She sighed again, muted the TV and placed the magazine on the coffee table. With seemingly nothing else to do, and obviously jaded, she looked at her smartphone on the table as if willing it to ring. She then picked it up as if to say *'what the heck'* and then started dialing a number from memory. All this time Adam was watching her intently and snapping pictures and was instantly captivated by her smile as he watched her dialing, wondering for an instant who she was trying to reach. He was now by the window, crouched underneath where he could almost touch it.

Instantaneously, the phone in his pocket started ringing. It was so sudden, so unexpected that he almost jumped from where he was hidden—which would have been unwise, because he would have been fully exposed and his quarry would have seen him. Instead, he quickly fished it out from his pocket, fumbled a bit, but somehow managed to mute the ringtone, and put it on vibrate. But he had enough time within that split second to see Lucille Yvette Young's face on the screen of his phone, smiling at him. *She had been calling him*!

Inside the house, Lucy also heard the ringing just outside the window, which apparently startled her because she immediately looked up, at the same time not sure if the sound was real, or if it was her imagination playing tricks on her.

She stood up, the phone still in her hand, and calmly and yet cautiously went to the window, her heart thumping. Her drapes were open, something she always did, and she scanned the darkness wondering if she had indeed heard a phone ringing as she was making a call, or if it was her mind playing tricks on her. Lucy scanned the dark surroundings again with her eyes before pulling the curtains shut. If she had glanced just below her window seal, she would have seen the last person she would have expected to see at that moment.

On the other hand, crouched just beneath, Adam lay still. His heart was pumping so hard that for a moment he was overwhelmed by a terrible fear that Lucy could hear it. After she stepped away and shut the curtains, he waited a moment longer, then crawled away after making certain that there was no one around—or worse, still watching him.

Finally, after an excruciating two and a half minutes, he was safely on the quiet street and headed back to the corner where he had parked his car—a rental, really, which he'd gotten three days earlier for $159 a day at a high-end car rental agency on Walnut Street in Pasadena. The vehicle was a diamond black 2006 Porsche Carrera.

Besides knowing that his time was almost up, Adam figured, why not splurge a bit? Under normal circumstances, he could have afforded to buy it outright in a matter of days. Business was good, and just recently, he and his partner had been awarded a lucrative contract providing pictures for a coffee book table. They could travel to any place in the world, if they so wished, to capture the pictures that would be spread in the glossy colored pages, and before the headaches became an issue, Paris had been the likely destination. Again, not for the first time, Adam wondered why life could have such a cruel sense of humor. He was on the verge of the breakthrough of a lifetime when everything seemingly fell apart.

He also knew that in this neighborhood, a Porsche would not attract unwanted attention from the local police, or even the sometimes overzealous private security guards who, to fight boredom during their regular patrols, would find nothing more fun to do than jostle a person who did not belong in the area. It was for this reason that he was not driving his regular car, a 2000 Toyota Camry.

Adam knew, though, that he was breaking one of the doctor's strict rules. In his state, given that he was now predisposed to seizures, he was not supposed to drive. But like everything else, including the possible danger of stalking Lucy, the warning had gone out the window. On the other hand, with this latest close call … there had been a few of them. Like when he took a picture of her while she was in the fruit aisle of a local Trader Joe's on Arroyo Parkway in South Pasadena, when an alert employee stopped short of asking him why he was secretly snapping pictures of a customer, though a smile from him was enough to keep the employee's curiosity in check. Once again, his good looks had come in handy. He now knew that he had pushed his luck far enough, and it was time to pull back a bit. Besides, he thought gleefully, she had called him after all.

Inside her apartment, after backing away from the window and sitting back on her loveseat, Lucy realized that her phone was still on all this time and she had yet to leave a message because her party, in this case Adam, had not answered. She pressed the 'end' button and called again. This time the call went straight to voicemail, with the generic answering machine telling her to leave a message after the beep.

"Oh, hi Adam, this is Lucy Young from the Coffee Gallery, hope you still remember me." She chuckled uneasily. "Just calling to see how you're doing. Call me back when you get a chance. *Ciao*!" she said before hanging up.

Later that night as she lay on her queen-size bed reading a paperback, something she did every night before going to bed, she could not help but wonder about the ringing sound she thought she'd heard outside her window earlier. Hard as she tried, she could not dismiss the thought. She told herself that it most likely was been a neighbor passing by, but even then, she was not totally convinced.

CHAPTER 8

BACK AT HIS APARTMENT, in the safety of his living room, Adam was scanning through the pictures he had taken on his most recent venture, still reeling from the close call he had just encountered. He dreaded to think what would have happened if Lucy had just tilted her head a few inches below her chin. The thought was enough to make him shudder. To take his mind off the near fiasco, he studied the pictures.

He had used a high-definition digital camera this time and could instantly view the images on the screen of the camera, one after the other. There was a picture of Lucy leaving her car, groceries in hand, and talking on her phone; a number of them in her living room, her kitchen, her bedroom, and so on. He did, however, draw the line somewhere. Tempting as it was, he could not bring himself to snap pictures of her undressing.

He thereafter connected the camera to a compact, yet expensive-looking printer which soon began spitting out the glossy eight-by-ten pictures he had selected. They were very beautiful, in spite of the poor lighting, he admitted to himself with a smile. He gently picked them up, one at a time, making certain not to smear his fingerprints on them—all thirty-five of the best—and took them to his second bedroom. The 'Dark Room,' as he liked to call it, one that even his maid was not allowed access to and was always kept locked.

There was a vast difference in the room this time around. On the far end of the room to his left, the entire length of the wall was arrayed with pictures, all of them of Lucy Young. Many of them had been taken from a distance, perceptibly with a telephoto lens attached to the camera. There were pictures apparently taken on different days, pictures of Lucy engaged in all sorts of different activities, totally unaware that she was being followed.

Fundamentally, her whole day-to-day routine could be discerned and dissected by merely studying the pictures. There were photos of Lucy shopping, Lucy at the gym, Lucy talking to different people, including friends; in other words, a day in the life of the lovely Lucille 'Lucy' Yvette Young. And tonight, as Adam admired the images with a smile on his face, another chapter was about to be added.

'Lucy at home', he thought to himself as he added the latest batch of pictures with a smile, totally pleased with himself as he lit a candle. There were a number of them around the altar of the shrine he had created, and he sat on a miniature stool he had specifically placed for what he was about to do—and that was to gaze at the different pictures in deep thought, for hours on end. This was his purpose now, for the pictures made him forget about his impending demise. They gave him strength, and they were like oxygen in his lungs. Gazing at the pictures also kept the insufferable pain at bay; or they did at least for a moment, and a moment was all he asked for.

As he was about to finally settle on the stool and prepare himself to do that for the next few hours, a thought suddenly came to mind and he smiled to himself in the dark. "Of course," he muttered to himself, and wondered why he had not thought about it sooner.

In his excitement he stood up quickly, knocking over the stool in the process, and in doing so he was hit with a terrible pain that shot up to his temples and blurred his vision. Before he knew it, he was on the floor the moment he was hit by a massive dizzy spell. It was when he was seated on the carpet of his dark room, massaging his temples as he gritted his teeth, that Adam once again pondered over his mortality—something he had gracefully forgotten when his mind and every grit of his being was focused on Lucy Young, the object of his affection.

As he slowly staggered to the bathroom to find the morphine, he had to ask himself the difficult question: *"What now?"* Would it be fair to take Lucy with him to the other side? Though he barely knew her, the little that he knew was enough for him to convince himself that whatever lay on the other side of mortality would not be worth facing without her.

The guilt hit him hard as he administered the drug through his vein inside his left elbow with a needle. He watched the blood shoot up in the syringe as it mixed with the clear liquid, and just as fast, disappear through the plunger and into the vein. It did not take long for him to start feeling the effects of the powerful painkiller. His head cleared, and with it the nagging pain that a few minutes later was replaced by a feeling of total bliss.

A few minutes later, he was relaxed and seated on his sofa in his living room. An imperceptible grin ran across his face as he began dialing a number on his smartphone.

The phone rang a few times before the throaty, and at the same time velvety and melodious, voice on the other end answered with a soft, "Hello?"

Oh, my sweet Lucy! Adam thought to himself before he cleared his throat.

"Oh, hi, Lucy."

"Hi, Adam." He could hear the sweet smile in her voice.

It was not lost on the love-struck young man that she had instantly recognized his voice, and with that his imagination was further inflamed. That meant she liked him, right? What else could it be? The fact that very few people in this part of the world had heard his accent never occurred to him. He was so caught up in this fantasy that he did not realize there had been an awkward pause.

"I saw a missed call from you and haven't had time to check my messages," he prevaricated. "Did you try calling me?"

"I did, as a matter of fact," Lucy said, and again she thought of the ring tone she heard outside her window right at the time when she was attempting to reach him. But of course, she never made the connection that he had been hiding right underneath her window seal, so she once again dismissed the thought. It had been a figment of her imagination. "I was checking on you," she continued. "Are you all right?"

"Yes, Lucy. I am feeling much better now, thanks." He wasn't lying about that; the morphine had now kicked in full-force.

There was another awkward pause as Adam thought of how he was going to phrase what he was about to ask her. He *had* to make her agree, because if she refused, that would crush him. It would ...

"Adam," Lucy called out, snapping him out of his reverie.

"Oh yes, sorry. I'm still here. That was very nice of you to check on me, Lucy." The grin that played on his face was wide as he cleared his throat, his mind racing six ways to Sunday. What he was about to ask her was very unusual for someone he'd just met, but then again he thought of the six weeks he had left, and figured he had nothing to lose.

Again there was another "Adam?" from the other end. The conversation, what little of it there was thus far, was becoming strained.

"Lucy, I know we just met, but can I ask you for a huge favor?"

Back at her apartment in her bedroom, Lucy rolled from her bed, brushed a strand of hair from her forehead, and sat up. She had been lying on her back when she received a call from him.

He's gonna ask me if I have a boyfriend, but he's gonna sugarcoat it first, she thought. Typical. Being an attractive woman, there had been no shortage of suitors. They came in all shapes and sizes, even married men, and so far she had rebuffed them all. But this one was different; very different, in fact. Not because he was foreign, but there was something about him—a lot about him, in fact—that she found herself very attracted to. But that did not mean she would make it easy for him, and thus lose his respect.

"Yes, I guess," she sighed. "What's up?" she asked in a feigned bored tone.

Adam paused for a brief second, gathering the courage to say what he was about to say.

"Can I take a few pictures of you? I think you would be a great theme. Not for the public, you understand, but you're … you look very photogenic."

Lucy smiled, turned over on her queen-sized bed, and lay on her belly as she folded her legs at the knees. She suddenly liked where this was going, and decided to have a little fun while they were on the subject.

"I guess. Now, do I have to take off my clothes and wear a thong?" she teased.

Not knowing if she was kidding or not, Adam decided to play it straight. What she said made a jolt of electricity run through his body, but the professional, the soul of a photographer, took precedence.

"Oh no, no, Lucy," he said quickly, "nothing like that. Just ..."

"You know I'm just kidding, Adam," she interrupted, laughing.

Nothing like a beautiful girl with a sense of humor to boot, Adam thought as he managed a chuckle of his own, albeit awkward.

"I was thinking more like pictures around landmark features in and around Pasadena and Altadena. You can then keep the ones you like, and hey, if part-time modeling is something on the horizon for you, you could use them. I'm sure you will not be disappointed," he said.

"Is that right, Mister Adam Mashabela?" she teased again. The woman was just simply amazing. If she had been there with him having a face-to-face conversation, Lucy would have witnessed the toothy grin that crossed his face. Above all, the way his last name rolled off her tongue was enough to give him chills. From her mouth to his ear, it sounded like *'Mar-Shar-Bell-Ah'*. Not even the trumpets from the archangels would have sounded any better.

"That's right, Miss Lucille Yvette Young," he threw it right back at her.

Lucy also giggled, but then froze for a second as she wondered whether she did in fact tell him her middle name, but just as quickly dismissed the thought. They had talked a lot that day at the Coffee Gallery and covered a lot of things, so it was quite possible that the issue about her middle name had come up.

In truth, she never did. Adam had found out more about her than she would have guessed at the moment. Undeniably, this was the electronic age with social media like Facebook, LinkedIn, Twitter, Instagram and the like, so it was easy to get information about anyone or anything. But as a person well-versed with the dark web, he'd dug up information not known by even her best friends.

"When were you thinking of doing this, Adam?" She was all business now, and he was momentarily caught off guard, but he recovered quickly.

"When do you have time? I am pretty much open," he announced, at the same time fighting to keep the excitement out of his voice. The thought of seeing her, meeting her legitimately without stalking her, was overpowering.

Lucy thought about this for a moment. "Let's see, it's Friday tomorrow. How about Saturday, early to late afternoon? Will that work for you, Adam?"

Would it ever! Only a broken back—or death, a far more real possibility in his case—would keep him from fulfilling this assignment. The only question now, and this was a tough one, was could he hold on for one more day? One day to keep himself from following her around on Friday and losing everything if she found out what he was up to—that being he had been stalking her unremittingly, and unobtrusively taking pictures of her? Right now, that was the one million dollar question. Lucy was like some wild acid trip to which he had to come running whenever it called. In the end, he figured that playing it safe would be the most prudent course to take. He could hang on to dear life for at least twenty-four hours, or slightly more.

On Friday he could use the time to map out the day, figure out the best spots to take her to, the different cameras to use, and factor in the aspects of the day such as the weather, the lighting, and so on. He could also catch up on some work at the studio. Besides, if the pull to see Lucy became unbearable, as it seemingly was with each passing day, he could always go to the shrine he had created of her. Again though, the troubling thought was that his six weeks were now down to five. Time was running out at an alarming rate. The clock was ticking, and the ticks grew louder with every hour.

"Perfect, I can come get you. I have a nice ride," he said. Modesty had long ago gone out the window with Adam Mashabela, the moment he found out that his life was measured now in weeks and days, instead of decades.

"Okay, Adam, let's do this. Kinda exciting, you know?" That enchanting soft titter again.

"Great," Adam announced. "I will be there at noon. Also, bring a change of your favorite clothes."

"Nice. Anything else?"

Gosh, she will be easy to work with, Adam thought. Normally at this point in the conversation, models would ask how much they would be paid and start the arduous process of negotiating and haggling, but he never faulted them. This was their livelihood, and they needed to be paid just like everyone else who rendered their services. But not his beloved Lucy. In her case, the reward would be out of this world, Adam had decided. She just did not know it yet.

"No, just you. Does noon work for you?"

"It sure does."

"Okay, great. Goodnight, Lucy." He would have loved to chat more, open up to her, tell her *everything*—but he knew that now was not the time, much as he wanted to. Instead, he caught himself before adding something stupid like '*see you in my dreams.*' Their relationship, or whatever he may have wanted to call it, had not reached that stage yet. He knew he would be pushing it, but hopefully after the shoot, their affiliation would move to a romantic dimension – he desperately yearned for that.

Lucy was just about to hang up when she remembered something very crucial.

"Adam, wait. Don't you need my address?"

He froze! Completely caught on the hop. A cold sweat broke out at the back of his neck and stung in his armpits. He could not tell if it was the morphine, or if he was caught in the excitement of meeting face-to-face, or both. Adam would have shown up on her doorstep on Saturday, and the question she would surely ask would be how on earth he knew where she lived. Right there and then, she would know that something was wrong in Denmark – she would get the first whiff that he had been following her.

"Huh?"

"You need to know where I live in order to come get me, right?"

There was a trace of alarm in her voice, something he was hearing for the first time, but the young man rallied nicely.

"Oh my goodness, yeah, you're right. I was so caught up in thinking about Saturday that I totally forgot – it's been a long day, Lucy." And to keep up the charade, he added, "Hold on, let me get a pen and paper." He then let a few seconds pass before he said, "Okay, I'm ready. What's your address?"

She gave it to him, and after she hung up, he heaved a heavy sigh. He was making mistakes; mistakes that would cost him dearly. He needed to slow down, he told himself.

CHAPTER 9

THEIR STUDIO IN OLD TOWN PASADENA was located on Raymond Avenue, one block south of Colorado Boulevard in what used to be an apartment building, which had since been converted into high-rent office spaces. How they managed to secure the place was in itself an interesting story. Steven Basa's uncle was an attorney and had won the office space in a medical malpractice lawsuit against the former owner, and since he had no real use for the place, he let his nephew and Adam rent it from him for a paltry sum of $550 per month. A steal, considering that the average rent for any commercial space in the area ran in the tens to fifty thousand dollars a month.

In its original form, the studio had been a two-bedroom apartment. What used to be the living room was their main office, reception area, and a place where they initially met prospective clients. The area was nicely furnished with a fireplace, two leather couches that faced each other from both ends of the room, with a rug that ran in between, and a coffee table with a glass top. The main desk that they both used was in front of a large window offering a wonderful view of the main buildings that were part of Old Town, the old train station. Further east was the beautiful mountain range that was Mount Wilson, clearly visible because their office was on the fourth floor of the building.

One of the rooms that had been a bedroom was where they kept their tools of the trade. Cameras, lenses, tripods, light umbrellas, and all the bells and whistles that came with the craft of professional photography. All five rooms in the studio had a different color paint, which gave the place a cozy and artistic feel to it. And as intended, clients—be it models, company executives or their representatives, or even aspiring actors needing a headshot for their resumes, electronic or hardcopy—were almost always impressed with the place.

This Friday morning, Adam caught an Uber to the office instead, and found his partner already at work. It seemed to Adam that his friend Steven practically lived at the studio. This morning he found him in the other room bent at a long work bench, studying an array of colored and black-and-white miniature photographs he had taken through a magnifying glass that he held with his right hand, as he panned from one picture to the next, each time grunting with satisfaction or disapproval.

In their line of work, attention to detail was the creed and lifeblood. What was normally missed by the ordinary person gawking at a picture or photograph was to them the difference between ordinary and extraordinary – a Pulitzer Prize winner, or something that would end up in a magazine or book editor's slush pile. It was that, timing, and a bit of luck, like being in the right place at the right time, camera in hand.

Their walls were covered entirely with many framed pictures of major historic events and prize winners, like John Filo's Pulitzer Prize winning photograph of Mary Ann Vecchio, a 14-year-old runaway, kneeling over the body of Jeffrey Miller minutes after he was fatally shot by the Ohio National Guard on May 4, 1970, when the National Guard opened fire on the Kent State University students who were peacefully protesting the war in Vietnam. Four students, all of them unarmed, including Miller, were killed with dozens more injured, some severely. One of them had ended up in a wheelchair for life.

There was a picture of Marines raising the American flag at Iwo Jima, a Vietnamese napalm attack, federal agents grabbing a boy at gunpoint inside a home in Miami. And there was one that was the first people saw when they walked into their office, for it faced the front door.

This was the picture taken on a day in November 1963 in Dallas, when news photographer Bob Jackson watched nightclub owner Jack Ruby shoot and kill presidential assassin Lee Harvey Oswald – inside police headquarters.

"He fired, and I hit the shutter ..." Jackson told the '*Denver Post*' in 2013. "I *couldn't have planned it any better.*"

The picture is well known. A wide-eyed Texas detective leaning back in surprise. Ruby pulling the trigger, and Oswald – eyes closed, mouth open – being shot at point-blank range.

There was also a picture that had almost caused a rift between the two friends, because they could not agree on its placement. Steven wanted it in the main office, but Adam vehemently objected, because its content was disturbing for the simple reason that it brought to the forefront the brutal truth of hunger, starvation, and death, all in one. It was the photograph known the world over as '*The Vulture And The Little Girl*' taken by the South African photojournalist Kevin Carter, which depicts a frail, famine-stricken girl collapsed in the foreground with a vulture eyeing her from nearby. She was reported to be attempting to reach a United Nations feeding center in Ayod South Sudan, somewhere in March 1993. Aside from winning the Pulitzer Prize for feature photography in 1994, it was also chosen as picture of the year by *American Magazine*.

Being African, born and raised, Adam Mashabela had witnessed firsthand the devastating effects of hunger, poverty, and illness, and this picture had hit close to home, which was why he found it very unsettling. They agreed as a compromise to hang it instead in the storage room, where he would not have to see it all the time.

Like everyone else, Adam knew that photography was a powerful medium. It can expose truths and show emotions that words never could. It can turn a mirror to our deepest fears and give us hope for humanity, and it can change the world – this, Adam Mashabela believed. However, there were some lines that could not be crossed, Pulitzer Prize or not, like openly displaying the disturbing picture of the little girl and the vulture at his place of work. And even resisting the urge to snap pictures of Lucy Young undressing.

These were the thoughts that were going through Adam's mind the moment he unlocked the door to his studio, stood in the middle of the nicely furnished room, and did a slow double-take of the place. It was like he was seeing it for the very first time. Not surprising, as life had taken a new and profound meaning. Things that he had always taken for granted, like the studio he and Steven had built from the ground up. He marveled now at the way he and his friend had accomplished in less than five years what took people in this line of work an entire career to realize, if at all.

He had come to terms with the fact that very soon he would be gone, and all this would be left to his friend. Adam knew that he would be leaving most of his life's work in very capable hands. Even on his own, Adam knew that his partner would raise their studio to heights they could only have dreamed of. It just saddened him that he wasn't going to be there when that happened, but he was slowly but surely coming to peace with his fate.

From where he was standing in the main room, he could see Steven through the slightly cracked door in the other room, still bent over the bench studying the photos. He had not, even for a moment, glanced up to acknowledge his friend and business partner's presence, despite the fact that he had not seen him for the past three days.

Instead, still stooped over with the magnifying glass to his eye, he asked, "So how did it go with Dr. Muhammed?"

Adam knew what he was inquiring about. His friend wanted the full details. It then occurred to Adam that close as they were, he could not bring himself to tell him the dreadful news. It would only serve to ruin what promised to be a good day for his beloved friend. Steven Basa, aside from being a workaholic like him, was a very vivacious, witty, jolly, and an all-around man about town who almost always found humor in anything—which was why it was always a pleasure to be around him, let alone work together. So, no, he could not burden him with the news of his impending death just yet. And as if on cue, the tumor said 'hello' again.

He winced and then gently rubbed his temples. This seemed to do the trick. That and a bit of morphine, of which he had taken a small dose that morning before coming to the office. The pain subsided, and Steven did not seem to have noticed that brief but rather prolonged pause before his friend finally gave an answer.

"It went well," Adam lied, "but the doctor still has to conduct more tests," he added rather quickly, as if attempting to halt any questions that may be forthcoming.

"I see," Steven said, looking up at last. His brow was twisted as he looked at his friend. "And the headaches, the dizzy spells, and the blackouts?" the Philippine wanted to know.

He had witnessed one of those dizzy episodes, and the blackout that followed, right there in their office, and it was not a pretty sight. It was an experience he never wanted to live through again. It had scared the living daylights out of him.

"He gave me something for that," Adam said almost dismissively. He was anxious to get off the subject, because it reminded him of his mortality.

Steven placed the magnifying glass on the table and walked over to his friend. He was a bit short, five feet five compared to Adam's six-foot frame, and was a bit on the chubby side with a round, jolly face.

He patted Adam on the shoulder and said, "That's good to know, Adam, because there's something I would like to run by you."

Adam had an inkling of what his friend had in mind. He had been hinting at it for the last few weeks before the headaches began. But before Adam could respond, Steven raised a finger and went to the kitchen. He opened the refrigerator, took out some margarita mix and a chilled bottle of tequila, and fixed drinks for the both of them—

even though Adam's margarita was the virgin kind, which meant it had no alcohol. However with Steven Basa it was business as usual. The man loved his booze.

He handed Adam his glass, the two silently toasted one another and then sat at opposite ends of the room, on the leather couches that faced each other. They normally did this when they had serious business to discuss. In the old days, when they could barely make ends meet and had to scrape for jobs, this would be a dreaded moment. Because of the crushing overhead, they would seriously wonder if they would survive the next month without closing shop. Thankfully those days were over now, and they were just about to get into a wonderful routine when the headaches began to crash the party.

Adam took a sip, his mind elsewhere, and then immediately shut his eyes and rubbed his temples. On seeing this, Steven sat up on his chair and studied his friend carefully, not liking what he was seeing.

"You all right man?"

It took a few seconds, but the pain soon subsided, "I am fine," Adam said between clenched teeth.

Steven nodded as he wondered if this was more serious than what Adam had led him to believe. However, after a while and noticing that the pained expression on his friend's face had disappeared, he said, "Adam, we've been doing quite well for the past couple of years, wouldn't you agree?"

Adam nodded, agreeing with the man. Steven then went into a long, tiresome, mind-numbing narrative about how he wanted to expand their venture into independent filmmaking, to start with a shoestring budget of $50 to $100,000, whatever the hell that meant. Clearly it was a very high-risk venture because they would be staking a huge portion of their working capital, meaning that if they could not recuperate the money invested within a timely period, they would sink—a possibility that did not seem to bother Steven at all. Of the two, he was always the risk-taker when it came to business. With Adam the risks lay in everything else, like stalking a woman he was in love with. And on and on he went, until it began to sound like gibberish to his ears.

In the end they agreed to revisit the matter in a week, after Steven finished reviewing screenplays that had been sent to him and 'weed out' those that did not have commercial appeal. Apparently he had already begun the process before he had even discussed his plans with Adam, who it seemed to Steven did not mind at all. His mind was elsewhere, it seemed.

Toward the end of their meeting, it was increasingly obvious to Steven that his friend was distracted and seemed eager to leave.

"What's going on, Adam?" Steven wanted to know, his brow twisted with utmost concern this time. Something was amiss, even though he could not tell exactly what that was, but something was wrong with his friend, very wrong. That much was clear. He had to wonder again whether Adam was more ill than he was letting on, and if so, how serious his illness was. It never occurred to Steven that his friend and business partner, a man he had been through a lot with, was terminal.

"How do you mean?" Adam tried to deflect with a weak smile, but the handsome young Motswana was fooling no one.

"You've been fidgeting, like distracted, your mind is all over the place. Like you did not hear a single word of what I've been saying. Are you sure you're okay, man?"

"I met a girl, Steve," Adam blurted out in a way that seemed more dramatic than it really was. This, he knew, would get his friend's attention and serve as a clever distraction to his mounting concerns.

To which Steven Basa exclaimed with a wide grin, "Ah!" as if that explained everything.

"And I'm taking her out on a shoot tomorrow." Adam smiled proudly as he proceeded to tap on his smartphone and handed it over to his friend. On the screen was Lucy Young's smiling face, that to his experienced eye seemed to have been taken from a distance.

Steven laughed outright, more with relief as he studied the beautiful face. No wonder his friend was acting a little strange. Anyone would, he thought, when faced with the prospect of being lost in those stunning green eyes; something even he could instantly tell from the picture.

"That explains it," he said as he studied the picture one more time before handing the phone back to his friend. "Now I see why I haven't seen you for three days, and why you've been a bit jittery, not hearing a word of what I've been saying, and eager to get out of here the first chance you get," he continued, still laughing.

Adam went on to tell him about his encounter with the strikingly beautiful woman. There was a twinkle in his eye whenever he uttered her name; something he had not seen in his friend in all the years that they had known each other. In their line of work, they worked with actresses, supermodels—in other words, many beautiful women who came in all sizes and colors. But it had always been business as usual with Adam, always maintaining the air of a very professional photographer. This, however, was entirely new. Perhaps, Steven Basa thought to himself, it had to do with the fact that he'd met her outside of work.

"So, when do I get to meet this beauty?" Steven wanted to know.

"Well, I can bring her by tomorrow," Adam said. "I was going to show her my place of work anyway," he added.

Steven smiled, took a gulp from his glass and said, "I see." And then after a brief pause added, "Good for you, Adam."

The two talked for a little while longer, discussing future projects including the coffee table book project, but above all places that Adam could take Lucy for the photo shoot the next day.

CHAPTER 10

SATURDAY IN EARLY JULY, when the first streaks of the southern California summer began bearing down in earnest, was a day Adam Mashabela would never forget. It had begun simply enough, like any other ordinary Saturday morning. He took the needed dose of his morphine—it had become a habit now—and in anticipation of the day ahead, packed a few more doses in a hidden compartment of his camera bag to administer when needed.

With the top down, he drove the Porsche to a nearby car wash at the corner of Walnut and Hill in Pasadena, close to the high-end car rental agency where he had rented the car. He had extended his rental agreement so he could keep the car for at least a month, and had it steamed, hand-washed, and then waxed to a shiny new. With an extra $50 dollar tip to the gentleman attending to his car, the Porsche looked new and carried a nice fragrance he was almost certain Lucy would like.

He had hardly slept the night before, thus the anticipation he felt at the prospect of seeing the beautiful woman later that morning was palpable, and felt as though he could reach out in the air and touch it. To say he was exhilarated would be a gross understatement. He was beyond a state of euphoria. Even picking what clothes to wear had been a daunting task, before he settled on a pair of comfortable jeans, sandals, and a nice polo t-shirt.

This time with the top down—he could always bring it down when needed—he drove to Lucy's home with a thumping heart, wondering for at least the hundredth time how the day was going to turn out. As he slowly cruised the streets of Pasadena, he played one of Prince's songs, '*The Most Beautiful Girl In The World*', and smiled to himself. *How appropriate*, he thought. He had already texted her to let her know he was on his way, so he was expected, because she had responded almost immediately with a smiling emoji that she would be ready by the time he got there and for him to wait in the car, but he was to let her know the moment he was in her driveway.

Not long afterwards, the sports car pulled into Lucy's driveway and Adam paused, collecting his thoughts before letting her know that he had arrived and was waiting outside. He heaved a heavy sigh as he pondered the day ahead. The headaches, which had been getting worse lately, surprisingly seemed to have subsided a bit, and it felt good. He looked around and smiled. The place that had become familiar looked a little different at this time of day.

He took in his surroundings. It was a gorgeous summer morning, and in the trees around the property, birds sang their sweetest melodies as the branches swayed with the morning breeze. Adam closed his eyes as he appreciated the moment – life had new meaning now, more than it ever did before that fateful day when he visited Dr. Maurice Muhammed's medical practice. He now appreciated every aspect of it.

The sound of the front door opening broke him out of his daydream, and his heart stopped. She had on large sunglasses, but somehow that did not hide her beauty. Her hair was a bit different, he noted, but he quickly realized that it had been permed—most likely the day before; otherwise, he would have known. She was wearing a pair of faded cutoff jeans with a few holes in the thighs, and a white blouse that looked more like a tank top.

The instant she saw Adam in the car waiting, she smiled and unconsciously assumed an elegant pose with her hand on her hip. The other hand shouldered the bag she was carrying, her change of clothes, apparently. It then occurred to him that she was admiring the car and was visibly impressed. On realizing this, Adam inwardly congratulated himself for having the foresight to make a good second impression, but my God! he thought, she was so beautiful. Being a Laguna Beach native, and thus a 'California beach girl,' she had a nice tan.

He had his window open, so he heard her clearly when she said, "Wow, Adam, that's a nice ride. Planning on driving the girls crazy?"

She was being her playful self again, and for some reason, even though this was to be their second encounter, he found himself warming up to her sense of humor.

"Nah," he said, returning her smile. "Just one, and her name is Lucy Young. Know her?"

"You're so sweet," she said as she walked toward the car.

On seeing this, Adam quickly got out of the car, took the bag from her, and dutifully opened the passenger door. A Porsche looks slight from the outside, especially since the type Adam had was a two-seater, but it can easily swallow up to two people, one of them six feet and the other five foot seven.

After gently closing the door behind her, he opened the trunk, which for a Porsche is in the front, and gently placed her bag among the other gadgets he had brought along. The camera, still in its silver casing, was placed on the passenger seat behind the driver's seat. There were two such small seats at the back. As he was doing this, he kept one eye on the object of his affection. She was still impressed; he could tell.

It really was not the car Lucy Young was impressed with. After all, she was from a well-to-do, upper middle-class family, and having been born and bred in Laguna Beach, California, she had seen it all. The best that life had to offer, in as far as material gain. What impressed her was the fact that the ride alone told her that Adam was doing well for himself. That much was clear, and nothing made a woman feel more secure. That, and the fact that he had opened the door for her.

Lucy herself had also taken steps toward impressing her suitor. In spite of what she may have led Adam to believe, or any of her friends for that matter, she had been truly flattered when Adam offered to take pictures of her like she was some supermodel of the month. It had flattered the heck out of her.

That was why the previous day, she got off early from work, went to a hair salon and gotten a perm, thereafter had a manicure and pedicure, and then relaxed in a spa for a couple of hours before she got home. For a few hours she went through her wardrobe, where she was spoiled for choice as far as picking clothes for the next day's shoot with that young, handsome immigrant. So when she saw the car, the silver case at the back seat, and other items for the shoot, she knew that all that preparation had not been in vain. She hoped Adam liked her latest hairdo and was relieved when he not only noticed it but complimented her on it.

When he got back inside the car, Adam smiled as he looked at her again. Her fragrance was intoxicating, and for a moment he was lost for words. To get an even clearer view of her, he took off his sunglasses—she had since taken hers off when she got inside the vehicle—and as before, he was lost once more in those enthralling green eyes. It seemed to him that she was even prettier than he last remembered when she was this close.

"Thanks for taking the time to do this, Lucy," he said in almost a soft murmur.

Her beautiful glossy lips parted to say, "Glad to do it, Adam." The smile, the dimples – it was sheer magic.

Still captivated by her face, he asked, "Have you had breakfast? Russell's serves great food at this time of day."

"No, but I'm fine, Adam."

"That beautiful body is gonna need fuel, Lucy. Come on, let's go." He smiled at her as he turned the powerful engine and put the car in reverse. Lucy realized that the vehicle was a stick shift as he slowly backed out of her driveway, into the main street, and gunned away.

Established in 1948 and located in the heart of Old Town Pasadena, Russell's serves very good food at reasonable prices. Adam ordered a hearty breakfast that consisted of pancakes, waffles, French toast, and sausages, and he ate with an appetite, washing it all down with a glass of orange juice. He was pleased with the breakfast, because lately food had lost its taste. Lucy, on the other hand, had an omelet and a cup of coffee, but also tasted some of Adam's food, something that pleased him immensely. All this time they talked and laughed freely, like long-lost friends finally reunited after many decades.

As before, they talked about everything and nothing, depending on how one looked at it. It was as though they had never left the Coffee Gallery, the place where they'd first met only a few days before, and now it felt as if many years had flown by. They prattled on in spite of the curious and furtive glances they were getting from other patrons. The fact that they were an interracial couple was enough to cause a stare, but throw in the fact that they were very beautiful people, and some people were practically gawking with envy, admiration, and of course, jealousy.

When it was time to leave, Adam paid the bill with his credit card and left the waitress a healthy tip in cash. Lucy was once again taken aback by his generosity as he regaled her with stories of his growing up in Africa, and above all the politeness he had extended to the waitress and everyone else he came in contact with. This, Lucy noted, he did without even trying. It was evident that he had been raised with the proper teaching toward his fellow men, and women in particular. Her thoughts then turned a little selfish. If he was like that with total strangers, what would he be like with someone he genuinely liked—someone like her? Well, she had already seen that, but to her it was just the tip of the iceberg.

The gestures were subtle, but impactful nonetheless. Like opening the door for her wherever they went, pulling out a chair for her to sit, and the way each request was accompanied by a polite 'please' and 'thank you'; a courtesy he extended even to strangers like the waitress. She could tell that all this was not an act he was putting on for her; it was more like a reflex action. But most importantly he was a great listener, not one who just waited to talk. He was genuinely interested in hearing what she had to say.

However, the only thing that concerned her a great deal was that at least twice during breakfast, she saw him wince a bit as he gritted his teeth in what looked like genuine pain and subsequently rub his temples, even though he tried to create an impression that all was fine. She had seen him go through the same routine at the Coffee Gallery, though not as penetrating. She would then ask him if he was okay, and on those two occasions he quickly recovered and told her that he was fine, and that would reassure her. However, she did wonder what was causing this difficulty and gently suggested that he see a doctor soon; something he reassured her over and over that he would do.

Afterward, the day was simply magical. First off, Adam took her to his place of work, which happened to be a stone's throw away, claiming that he needed to quickly check his mail. In truth he wanted to show the place off, and show her off to his friend and partner. Both gambits worked. Lucy was totally impressed with the place, and Steven Basa was floored by her beauty, even rambling on about her being welcome anytime and any day at the studio.

She thanked him, amazed at the place. Adam had, of course, told her about the place enough that it had formed an image in her mind's eye, but seeing it in person was mind-boggling, to put it mildly, and in no uncertain terms she told the two gentlemen such. They soon left, but not before Adam and Steven took turns snapping a few pictures of her in various positions as a secretary, complete with reading glasses. It had been what Adam called 'warm-up shots' to give her an idea on how to 'communicate' with the camera. She was fast learning the whole jargon that came with professional photography.

From there he took her to the great City Hall of Pasadena, and took pictures of her first with the great dome in the background, and then a few of her by the water fountain, then some around the gigantic busts of two of Pasadena's most famous natives—the Robinson brothers, Jackie and Mack. Jackie Robinson was, of course, the first black baseball player to break the color barrier by playing for the Brooklyn Dodgers, later the LA Dodgers after their move to Los Angeles. He was not only inducted into the Hall of Fame, but also had his number '42' retired by all the teams in major league baseball. His brother Mack, an accomplished athlete in his own right and the elder of the two, had won a silver medal at the 1936 Summer Olympics held in Munich.

From here, he took pictures of her at the mirror pool at Pasadena City College on Colorado Boulevard, the Huntington Library, the Rose Bowl, and other such famous landmarks and places of interest. It became apparent to Lucy that Adam had done his homework. He was quick and efficient, with no time wasted. Every place was well mapped out beforehand. But most importantly, it did not take her long to realize that Adam was really good at what he did.

Every place, every landmark had a story behind it. Why it was called such and such, and why it was located in that area. The pros and cons of having that particular place in said area. For instance, the Rose Bowl, he told her, had for many years been a source of irritation for the surrounding neighbors because of the noise and traffic congestion it caused whenever there was an event like a concert, a football game and so on.

In fact, the famous stadium had hosted a few games of the 1994 FIFA World Cup, a worldwide soccer event that comes once every four years. The game, Adam took pains to explain, was huge the world over, and prior to 1994, the sport in the United States was less than a footnote. But of course the World Cup, also affectionately known as the '*Mundial,*' changed that.

He was the complete professional, she observed, and went out of his way to make her comfortable. Making the best of the situation, he never once disapproved of any of the clothes she had brought with her. Adam could have snapped photos of her wearing greasy work overalls worn by auto mechanics and would have found a theme for it. As a matter of fact, he had taken a few pictures of her posed in and around the Porsche with the sole intention of sending a set of the pictures to that vehicle's manufacturer in Germany, to perhaps pique their interest a little about using some of them, if not all, for marketing purposes. Certainly, if that were to happen, they would have to pay for them. And the model—in this case, Lucy—would be entitled to royalties of some sort, which he would personally see were was properly disbursed.

However, this was wishful thinking, any photographer's dream, because these multibillion corporations had their own public relations and marketing departments with their own photographers who took care of such matters. But once in a while, a random picture that put their product in great eminence did grab their attention, which is what Adam was hoping for by having the knockout of a woman pose alongside the Porsche. And that was why it was not uncommon to have these companies receive such unsolicited pictures.

For the final shoot of the day, they drove to Malibu Beach. The setting was perfect, because it was late in the afternoon when they decided to drive down there, this time with the top of the luxury sports car down. Once in a while, as he negotiated first the 10 freeway and then later the fabled Pacific Coast Highway, which ran along the Pacific Ocean, he would marvel at Lucy as the wind caught her hair.

By the time they reached their destination, the summer sun was already setting, and with it in the background, the photos he took of her were breathtaking. Lucy among the rocks, Lucy clad in a string bikini and matching bra posing on the sandy beach, sunglasses on, another of her pretending to handle a big crab. Lucy reading a paperback, sunglasses on in one and another without; there was also one with her elegantly posed in a straw hat. And best of all, one of Lucy, her back turned to him, walking parallel to the waves and leaving footprints behind her.

All this drew much attention, of course, and she was loving it even though she tried to be nonchalant. Adam could not help but suppress a grin of satisfaction. The spectators saw in her what he had seen – a very beautiful and gorgeous woman. Some young women during brief recesses, especially when Lucy had to go into one of the public restrooms to change into something else, would ask Adam if his services were for hire and even offer their phone numbers, and in some cases business cards, all of which were politely rebuffed. This was Lucy's moment, and hers alone. With many, it was easy to tell that it was the photographer they were interested in, and not his art.

They wrapped up the day with dinner at the famous Malibu Pier; the day had been a roaring success. The restaurant they chose, The Malibu Farm Café, is located in a midcentury café at the end of the pier and features farm-fresh local and organic foods. So they stepped in, ordered their food at the counter and grabbed a seat on the reclaimed picnic benches inside by a window, where even at that time of the day, they could see surfers and dolphins in the water at First Point.

After making sure that Lucy was comfortable, Adam excused himself and went to the men's room. He had earlier on unobtrusively retrieved the syringe and bottle of morphine he had hidden in his camera bag, and put them in the fanny pack around his waist. The pain, which he had thus far kept at bay, was coming back in waves, and he now needed to administer the drug.

Inside one of the stalls, he sat on the toilet seat, cover down, and after making certain that the latch on the door was secure, he filled the syringe with the painkiller and, injected it into his vein. Then he sat for a while as he felt the drug work its magic. He grabbed a good amount of toilet paper, and with it covered the used syringe and the tiny empty bottle that had contained the liquid painkiller. On his way out, he casually tossed it in the waste bin by the door.

He got back to find Lucy already inspecting a tray with a plate of farm scrambled eggs and salmon, with a side of ricotta, baby potatoes, and country wheat toast. Adam's food, which had also arrived in his absence, was a skirt steak with country wheat, lemon aioli, arugula, tomato, red onion, and black and white rice. The drug in his blood heightened his senses, apparently, because the food smelled really great as he took his place on the other side of the table. A candle was burning in the middle, and as such, the setting was romantic.

Adam smiled at her and said, "Don't you just love it when you come back and find the food already at the table?"

She looked up from her plate and offered a slight smile for an answer. Adam sat down and said a silent prayer, as he had been taught to do by his grandmother, but then after the first bite it occurred to him that Lucy was suddenly and unusually quiet.

101

When he looked up and saw tears welling in her beautiful eyes, the young man was instantly distressed.

"D-did I say something wrong Lucy?"

She shook her head 'no' and proceeded to do something totally unexpected. A move that, for at least the second time that day, made his heart stop. Lucy stood up slowly, tears still flowing down the smooth skin of her cheeks, and making no attempt to wipe them off whatsoever, walked up to where he was seated, sat next to him and ceremoniously threw her arms around him in a warm and distinctly affectionate embrace.

"Oh, Adam," she moaned softly, her lips actually touching his ear lobe. "Thank you for such a wonderful day. You made me feel so special."

"Lucy ..." He tried to speak, but she silenced him by placing a well-manicured finger on his lips.

"Shhhh," she cooed as she planted a long and wet, passionate kiss on his lips, to which he responded dutifully. And that's when it exploded between them—the passion, the ecstasy, and the joy that had been bottled up, waiting just beneath the surface to explode like a volcano. Their meal was instantly forgotten, and with it their appetite.

Their romance had begun, and for the moment everything was forgotten. Even the dreadful news he knew he would have to reveal to her, that being he was not long for this world.

CHAPTER 11

THEY WALKED OUT OF THE MALIBU FARM CAFÉ hand in hand, and the feel of her delicate touch and her body against his kept him in a constant state of electronic tingles. What he felt went beyond euphoria, beyond erotic, beyond any feeling he had ever experienced in his life, he told himself. Even thoughts of his impending death were, for the moment, forgotten – as of right now, that almost certainty felt as if it had never existed to begin with.

It was already nighttime when he opened the door to the car for her, and gently shut it the moment she was comfortably seated. They then drove off, but instead of making a right on the Pacific Coast Highway, which would have connected them to the 10 freeway heading east and eventually with the Pasadena freeway, Adam turned left instead.

There was a good reason why he chose to do so. A full moon was out, and as they drove along the Pacific Coast Highway with the ocean to the left, the reflection of the moon on the dark ocean was the stuff fairy tales are made of. It was simply magic, if not enchanting. Keeping within the speed limit, and playing love ballads as they spoke and admired the view of the moonlit ocean, was a moment they both wished would never end. And when the 1970s classic song 'Lucy' by The Commodores came on, something Adam had pre-arranged, *his* Lucy actually shed a tear and tucked her left arm under his, and rested her head on his shoulder. For the next thirty miles they silently listened to the ballads that reached deep down inside them and touched something special.

It was 2:45 a.m. when he finally pulled into her driveway,. She had fallen asleep on his shoulder for most of the way back as the love songs played along. The way they sounded, the carefully selected songs from the iPod he had connected to the car's stereo system seemed as if the lyrics had been written specifically with the two young lovers in mind, and the irony of songs like 'Lucy', 'Lady You Bring Me Up When I'm Down', and 'Start Of A Romance' was not lost on them.

Adam looked at the sleeping beauty still resting on his shoulder the moment he brought the vehicle to a stop. She was dead to the world, and he did not blame her. It had been a long, productive day, tiresome no doubt, but she had handled it like a true professional and he loved her all the more for that. She could have called the whole thing off halfway through the shoot and he still would have been satisfied. But she saw the whole thing through, following direction without question, and most of all without even asking for any monetary compensation; except for a copy of the pictures, from which she could pick the ones she loved the most.

He looked at her for a very long time, not wanting the spell to end. She looked peaceful and serene; like the calm and dark Pacific Ocean lit by a summertime moon they had just witnessed. Reluctantly, he gently nudged her awake, announcing that she was home. Lucy's eyes fluffed open as she looked up, dazed and confused by the light spilling through the windshield from the apartment's floodlights. Upon realizing where she was, at last she looked at her new man and smiled.

"I must have fallen asleep," she said as she stretched her arms and yawned.

"You sure did, Lucy." Adam returned her smile.

He helped her gather her things and walked her to the door, where they hugged once more and kissed, and promised to call one another the next day. Adam waited in the car to make certain that Lucy was safe and sound in her apartment before the luxury car engine roared to life and he drove away.

CHAPTER 12

THE NEXT MORNING, Lucy woke up to find a bouquet of a dozen long-stemmed red roses waiting for her at her doorstep. The roses were accompanied by a sweet note from Adam, thanking her profusely for taking the time to do the shoot, but that was not all. In a separate envelope tucked in the roses was a check written to her and drawn on his company's account, for fifteen hundred dollars. She was taken aback—not so much by the amount, which she thought was overly generous, but by the note which accompanied it, telling her to please accept it and not feel insulted, even though payment had not been discussed. But he'd stated categorically that he truly valued her time.

Even though Lucy had not expected monetary compensation, and at the moment did not really need the money, a girl could always use some extra cash. The fact was, she realized more than ever that Adam valued her as a person, and therefore treasured her time. Once again, and not for the first time, Lucy was astonished by the handsome young man from Botswana.

She picked up the flowers, sniffed at them with eyes closed, and once she was back inside the house she immediately reached for her iPhone on the glass coffee table in her living room and dialed his number from memory to thank him. The call was supposed to last a couple of minutes at the most, they both thought. Instead they ended up talking for hours on end, and once they were through, they were both astonished at the length of their call when three and a half hours felt like fifteen minutes.

And so it went. For the next three weeks, the two lovers either spoke on the phone or saw one another at the very least excuse. They went to the movies at the Santa Anita Mall in Arcadia, a plush suburb three miles east of Pasadena; they took long walks hand in hand. They visited the Huntington Library in Pasadena, walked the trails of Eaton Canyon, watched the sunset from Mount Wilson, and even took nice, long drives to places like San Diego, Venice Beach, and Santa Barbara. A trip to Las Vegas was planned, but then postponed because Adam all of a sudden did not feel well on the day they were supposed to leave.

That was the thing that concerned Lucy the most. On several occasions, she had watched Adam go through what to her looked like excruciating pain. He would all of a sudden gasp for air, eyes bulging, rubbing his temples using his forefingers, and then excuse himself by going to the nearest bathroom or someplace where he would be alone. He would be there for at least five minutes and then come out rejuvenated, as if nothing had happened. She had to wonder what that was all about, and whenever she asked, he succeeded in convincing her that it was nothing really, and blame it on overworking. Lucy had to wonder if that was true, though, on the occasions when she witnessed these seemingly painful episodes. Even though they had opened up to one another to some extent, she could not fight the feeling that there was something her new man was keeping from her. Not being a nosy person by nature, she decided to bide her time.

Fear only gripped Adam whenever he was alone with his thoughts in his apartment, especially at night as he would wander about aimlessly from one room to the next. He was still seeing Dr. Muhammed every other day, and taking his medication as instructed. The doctor had warned him that the seizures would start any time, followed by constant fatigue, and when that happened he was to notify him as soon as possible. Dr. Muhammed also gave him a device the size of a pager that he would have to press if he was incapacitated, and an ambulance would be dispatched immediately to his residence, and thereafter to the hospital. What the esteemed doctor did not tell him, but Adam guessed, was that when that happened, he would be kept at the hospital until the end.

This worried the young man. The clock was ticking, Lucy was madly in love, and so was he. Their bond grew stronger with every day that passed, and each day drew him ever so much closer to his mortality, and with it the resolve to spill the beans and reveal his deepest, darkest secret to her grew all the weaker. That was when he began having thoughts of taking her with him.

With this in mind, he began researching in earnest about the afterlife. He checked out books on the subject at the Altadena Library, which, thankfully, was within walking distance of his apartment. He even surfed the web, dark and regular, visiting sites that dealt with the subject. He had come to terms with *his* mortality, but Lucy now complicated things. The thought of leaving her behind and at the mercy of some tomcat who would later take his place was something very hard to contemplate, let alone imagine. But then again, Adam Mashabela was never an evil or selfish man, and he had to really think about this. Was taking Lucy fair to her? This was a question that kept him awake literally all night, wandering from room to room. He decided to shelve the thought until the time was right to make that crucial decision about whether he would kill Lucy or not, and that would be the night when he finally would, at long last, reveal his dark secret to her.

With that in mind, he knew the time had come to reveal the truth. How that was going to be received was anyone's guess, but one thing for certain was that it would be an ugly situation, there could be no avoiding that. He thought long and hard about how he was going to reveal the news to her. There was simply no way around it; whatever scenario he could come up with ended with nothing but grief for her, tears, and even more tears. But he would try to placate her like never before.

Adam then called Lucy and invited her to dinner at his apartment for the next night. He told her that he would prepare the meal himself, and that seemingly impressed her even more. She asked him again if he could really cook, and not anything from a takeout joint, to which his answer was:

"I can dazzle a bit, Lucy." His beloved grandmother back in Botswana had taught him well.

"Anything I can bring, or help you with the cooking in any way?"

The thought of him and Lucy in his cozy kitchen, aprons on, cooking, talking and laughing, basically having fun like never before, was very tempting indeed.

"Nah, I got everything handled. Just bring your pretty self along, and your appetite," he said, and to himself he thought, *I also got a nice little surprise for you.*

"Okay, darling, I will see you then," she said before hanging up. Lucy then smiled to herself. It had been a little over three weeks ago since they had made it official between them, and she intended on spending the night with him, even if she made the first move—which she was fully prepared to do. Adam just made her feel special more than any man she had ever known, and she was going to reward him with a blissful evening.

With that in mind, she contemplated what bottle of California wine she would bring.

⁓⁓⁓

The afternoon of the dinner date was a busy one for Adam Mashabela. After taking a little more than the required dose of morphine, which had become a habit now, he drove to a place called Michaels on Colorado Boulevard in Pasadena. Here, he bought mugs, placemats, a rolling pin, saucers, plates, and a plain white apron normally worn by professional chefs at five-star hotels and other such places.

He got more than subtle strange looks at a place called FedEx Kinko's, where he had different pictures of Lucy superimposed, first on the front of the white apron, which after being worn would have the beautiful smiling face of Lucy staring right back. He then had the pictures placed on the mugs, saucers, placemats, and rolling pin. The pictures used had been printed from his iPhone, and there had been many to pick from.

Adam could feel the curiosity of the young woman assigned to assist him grow with every second. She was too much of a professional to pry, but she was human after all, and in the end the human side won. Adam sensed it, and then decided to save her the trouble of asking.

"It is for a feature film we're making," he smiled.

The beautiful smile, of course, worked its intended magic and put her at ease, but now since he had opened the door, she decided to pry even deeper.

"Oh, wow," she exclaimed, visibly impressed. "What kind of movie?"

"Have no idea, I'm just a PA," he said.

"PA?"

"Yeah, Production Assistant. Not as glamorous as it sounds, because we're the ones at the bottom of the totem pole. You know, the errand boys, the guys they send for coffee runs, to pick up the mail, and all the odds and ends a producer or any of the other hard-hitting honchos would never be caught doing," Adam replied.

"Oh, I see," the young woman smiled as she nodded in complete understanding.

And that, thankfully, put her curiosity to rest. It was true, however. Production Assistants were sometimes regarded as lower than extras on a movie set, which is why the somewhat nosy employee felt there was no need to engage in any further discussion regarding this issue.

In the end, the bill came to $68.12. Adam peeled off four crisp twenty-dollar bills from his wallet and with a smile told her to keep the change, then quickly walked away, leaving the astonished woman behind him, who now had to wonder if the handsome young man with the strange accent was indeed a PA, and wondered yet again who the lucky woman in those pictures was.

CHAPTER 13

IN ANTICIPATION OF LUCY'S VISIT a little later that evening, Adam was busy setting up everything, making certain that the mood was just right. The light in the living room where they were going to cuddle on the sofa, wrapped in a blanket as they ate popcorn and watched a romantic movie, was dimmed just right, with soft music playing in the background.

Inside the kitchen, he had prepared a sumptuous meal that could have fed at least eight people. In this instance, though, Adam had more than outdone himself in a way that would have made his grandmother proud. There were baked potatoes, steamed rice, beetroots, steaks, roasted meat, dumplings, rich, thick steamy gravy made from diced tomatoes and fried onions, asparagus, mushrooms, and for dessert there was cream pudding, sliced peaches, and cake.

The table in the kitchen that could seat four, but was now set for two, was covered with a beautiful table cloth bought specifically for this moment, and on it were the placemats with Lucy's picture overlaid on them, momentarily hidden by the beautiful china plates that were set on them. In the middle of the table were two candles, which were to be lit once dinner was served and ready to be had, and a bottle of 2009 Chateau Latour Pauillac wine that cost $1,799.97, which he had since found out was Lucy's favorite; something he picked up in their seemingly never-ending conversations about their likes and dislikes. This was to be another one of the surprises he had in store for her.

He had been so busy preparing for this night that he barely had time to take a shower himself, and after he did, he realized that he had only fifteen minutes before her impending arrival. He quickly put on a pair of faded jeans with holes at the knees that he liked wearing when he was at home relaxing or working on an outdoor shoot during summer, a pair of black Nike slippers and a white Polo t-shirt, and over it he threw on the white apron which had the picture of a smiling Lucy emblazoned on the front. He then went back into his bedroom, starred at his reflection in the full-sized mirror, and nodded with satisfaction.

Adam had no idea what type of message this would send, but in his mind he thought it would be romantic. Especially in light of what he planned on revealing to her this evening. And as if on cue, his eyes fell on a book he had been reading over the past few days that he had checked out at the Altadena Library. It was a book about *'The Afterlife'* by a Doctor Michael Sabom, or something like that. Inside the book was a plain white envelope addressed to none other than Lucy Yvette Young.

He took the envelope out of the book and placed it neatly in the front pouch of his apron, which was a few inches beneath Lucy's picture. Adam was putting the final touches to the table when the doorbell rang ceremoniously. Immediately, and not for the first time, he cupped his hand and breathed into it to make sure that his breath was just right. He also sniffed at his armpits one at a time – all was good. The nice fragrance of the very expensive male perfume was performing as advertised.

Adam was just about to head to the living room when he suddenly remembered something, snapped his fingers, turned around and disappeared into the interior of his apartment. He reappeared a few seconds later, just as the doorbell chimed for a second time, and this time he was holding his beloved camera without the telephoto zoom lens posed dead center in the living room, camera in hand and ready. There was a wide grin on his face as he aimed at the door, ready to snap a picture of his lady love.

"Come on in," he said.

The door opened, and in entered Lucy Young, gorgeous as ever. The moment she did, the flash from the camera momentarily stunned her, catching her off guard, but to her credit she recovered quickly. She looked stunning in a short denim skirt, leather flip-flops, and a spaghetti striped sleeveless blouse. He had no way of knowing this, but she was not wearing any underwear, as this was the night she decided she was going to give herself to him. The thought alone was enough to give her body a jolt of electric current she had been feeling on her way to his place.

Lucy smiled but was not entirely surprised. She was already getting used to her boyfriend's dramatic tendencies, but was elated nonetheless. Adam had a way of making her feel exceptional, and this latest maneuver was just one of many. She could not help but wonder what else he had in store for her.

"Hey," she said as she smiled, trying to hide the fact that she had been taken aback.

She was about to say something more, but Adam interrupted her gently by saying, "I just thought I would capture this moment that will be forever etched in our memories. That, my darling, is the beauty of photography."

He then placed the Canon 5D Mark 111 camera on the glass coffee table in the middle of the living room and stood with his arms on his waist, appreciating the sight before him, and also in a not-so-subtle way making sure Lucy noticed her picture on the apron.

Lucy instead looked around the living room, as someone normally does when entering a home for the very first time. The place was immaculate for a bachelor and well kept. She remembered that he had told her he had a maid who came in every other day to clean up, which explained the not-so-subtle feminine touch to the place. It was also well furnished. The sofa and loveseat were black leather, she could immediately tell, and the walls had an array of beautiful paintings and framed photographs, one of which she noticed on the coffee table was of her. She then looked up at him in total appreciation, and that was when she noticed his apron and her smiling picture ogling right back at her.

He kissed her on the lips, took her purse and hung it on a coat hanger by the door, and then took a step back. The apron was again on full display, and Lucy studied it for a moment, not certain what to make of it. She smiled, albeit nervously, though she tried to hide it.

She reached out and touched it, and then said, "Wow … Adam, that's so sweet, but you didn't have to do that."

He smiled and said, "I thought I would liven up the mood a little. You know, this being our anniversary."

Lucy's brow twisted in slight bewilderment as she unconsciously took half a step back, and then asked, "Anniversary?"

Adam did not immediately answer, as he was now rubbing his temples. A wave of pain had suddenly hit him as he remembered that he had yet to take his morphine. The previous dose was beginning to wear off.

Lucy did not seem to notice, because she continued by saying, "It's been a month, Adam …"

"Six weeks, to be exact," he corrected her, now rubbing the right side of his temple with his forefinger this time.

He looked at her for a while, a bit glassy-eyed from the intense pain, as he wondered how she was going to receive the news about his imminent death. Not for the first time, he somewhat cursed himself for dragging this beautiful woman into what he could only describe as his own personal hell. However, he again consoled himself with the fact that what he had in store for her, the surprise gift in the envelope in the front pouch of his apron, would be more than enough to placate her.

Adam rubbed his temples again and closed his eyes as the tumor again said 'hello'. This time, Lucy took note.

"Are you all right?"

As if by reflex, startling her at the same time, he gently grabbed her by her elegant shoulders, drew her close to himself, and looked her right in the eye with an intensity that she had never seen before, but was strangely affectionate nonetheless.

"Just remember, Lucy," he said, still looking into her enchanting, bright emerald-green eyes that never failed to serve their purpose in captivating him, "*every* single day with you is worth a thousand years to me."

Deeply touched, she said softly, "Oh, Adam." And then placed her head on his chest.

They stayed that way for close to a minute; two people deeply in love. The spell was broken when Lucy suddenly looked up at him and said, "I heard that you went to see the doctor again today."

It was true, but as far as he knew, only one person besides Dr. Muhammed was privileged to that information, and that was his business partner.

To say this information jolted him would not be an exaggeration.

"Lucy, who told you that?"

She pulled away as she stroked a strand of hair behind her ear, and said in a way that suggested that it was no big deal, "Oh, your buddy at the studio, what's his name again?

"Steve?"

"Yeah, Steve. I stopped by to surprise you and see if you'd like to have a cup of coffee across the street." Just like him, she always counted the days, the hours, and minutes before seeing him. "Are you okay, babe? Because you seem a bit jittery tonight."

The irony of the century, Adam thought wearily. Aloud he said, "Oh, I'm fine, babe. Just some headache."

"Again?" Lucy asked, her brow twisted with concern. She had noticed that about her boyfriend ever since they took their relationship to a different level, the seemingly endless headaches. What was wrong with this beautiful man? She had to wonder. She intended to find out, especially since this was the night she intended to sleep with him for the very first time, and after that there would be no secrets. If there were any, she was determined to pry them out of him, either in spades or one at a time. She was not going to nag him, though. Lucy had long decided against that, plus it was not in her nature to be that way.

"Yes."

"Did the doctor tell you why you keep getting them?"

This was where things would get hairy. He could tell her the truth right here and now, and ruin a perfectly planned evening, get it over with, or he could wait. Either way, it would have to be tonight. How the truth was going to be received was not something he wanted to contemplate at the moment. The best thing would be to stall, feed the truth to her one bite at a time.

"Not really. They think I work too hard. stress, you know," he lied smoothly with a smile on his face, given mainly to diffuse the slight tension that was beginning to build. But Lucy was not easily dissuaded. It was the same lie each time.

"You should get a second opinion, babe. This is getting out of hand," she suggested.

Adam dismissed her concern with a wave of his hand and smiled once again. His charm always worked, but for some reason, tonight it was not getting the desired results.

"I wouldn't say that, Lucy darling. See, that's the problem with you people from the First World. You go to see a doctor for *everything*. In Botswana we just ride it out, no big deal."

"It's a big deal, Adam," she pressed on, and then she reached up and gently stroked the side of his chin with her hand, and cooed softly, "Promise me you will get a second opinion, babe. Okay?"

He sighed and closed his eyes—not because he was digesting the advice handed to him, but because another wave of pain had suddenly engulfed him. He opened his eyes after it passed, his gaze glassy.

"I will, sweetheart. I will."

She smiled, wiped a tear, and once again looked at her picture on his apron, then kissed him hard and long.

"You *always* make me feel special, my love. Thank you, Adam." She looked up again and said, "I couldn't bear it if something happened to you."

Adam felt as if a truck had hit him in the chest; her words were chilling. Not wanting this uncomfortable trend to continue, he gently held her by her elegant shoulders, drew her away from him and smiled. He knew he couldn't tell her that everything would be fine and that she wasn't going to lose him, because that would be a lie; not after what he was going to tell her before the night was over.

"Now close your eyes."

"What for?" she asked with a smile on her face.

"It's a surprise, Lucy," Adam's grin revealed every tooth, knowing that she would be intrigued.

"What is it I'm closing my eyes for?" she insisted, obviously anxious to find out what was in store for her and forego this juvenile game.

"Like I said, babe, it's a surprise that's surely going to blow your mind on this day, our six-week anniversary."

They were still in the living room, so Lucy took a step back and eyed him with a bit of curiosity for the first time that night—perhaps the first time in their relationship, for she was a bit perplexed.

"Oh, you've been counting?" she asked, as if the thought itself was unusual, as in fact it was.

"Yes, and this is a surprise that will change your life, Lucy. I swear to you. Now close your eyes, darling."

The toothy grin had yet to fade from his face. Lucy had to wonder if the surprise was in a black velvet box, and inside that box was an engagement ring. The thought alone was enough to cause her heart to lurch a bit. She loved him like no other, that much was true; but this was way too soon. She would have to let him down gently, she thought. But then again, she had to ask herself if she would ever find anyone who would love her as much as this man obviously did. What girl would pass up the chance of marrying the man of her dreams? A man who almost literally worshipped the ground she walked on?

Shaking herself out of her brief brown study, she returned the smile and softly said, "Okay." And did as she was asked.

Holding her gently by the shoulders, he guided her into the kitchen, totally missing a framed picture of her on the TV stand. In the kitchen, Lucy was greeted first by the smell of the food. She had long ago caught a whiff of it while in the living room, but now it was stronger and smelled even more delicious.

After making her stop, he said a bit dramatically, "*Voila* … you can open your eyes now."

When Lucy did, she was genuinely astonished by the sight on the small kitchen table. It was marvelous. Two candles set on opposite ends of the table, and in between was a lavish meal. There was steamed rice, baked potatoes, asparagus, steak, dumplings, rich gravy, and beetroots.

"Oh my goodness!" exclaimed a wide-eyed Lucy. "This is exquisite, Adam. I didn't know you could cook so well," she added, totally impressed and already feeling the saliva underneath her tongue.

On seeing the smile on the beautiful woman's face, the beam on Adam's face widened even further.

"You like?" he asked, still smiling with his arms widespread.

"Yes, I like. Totally," she said. "I'm really impressed, Adam. A surprise indeed."

He gently and methodically parked her on her chair. There was an empty plate in front of her, ready to be filled with food, and the chef in charge was ready to oblige her appetite.

"Oh no, this is *not* the surprise, my love," he said as he patted the pouch on his apron, took out the envelope with her name written on it, and then placed it on the table. "It's just the beginning."

He then opened the wine bottle, served some in a glass and handed it to her. Using a spatula, he served rice on her plate, a dumpling, asparagus, gravy, each time asking if what he was serving was enough. He then used a steak knife to cut the meat. To serve it, he had to lift her plate and bring it closer to the steak tray, and in doing so he exposed the placemat beneath it. Lucy froze. Her smiling face was staring right back at her.

"Eh, Adam, babe ... w-what's this?" she asked, pointing at the superimposed picture of her on the placemat. The smile on her face was replaced now with a look of concern, no doubt coupled with fear at the same time. There was love, and then there was unhealthy obsession. What Lucy was beginning to see bordered on the latter.

Adam, on the other hand, did not seem the least bit perturbed, not for a moment thinking that something like this could startle anyone. It was almost certain that the tumor had a lot to do with his sensible capabilities.

On seeing the worried look of his lady love, Adam put the plate back on the table, sat on a chair next to her, and took her hand in both of his. Just as he was about to open his mouth and say something, he was hit with yet another wave of pain that was acute enough to make him grit his teeth and close his eyes for a moment. This was not lost on Lucy. It wouldn't be an overstatement to say that Adam was acting strange.

"Oh, that?" Adam said in a way that made it sound as if it was no big deal, really. "That's so I can be with you, see you all the time, my love." He gritted his teeth again. This time the pain lingered a bit longer.

"But babe, you know you can see me whenever you want. You don't have to do this." She pointed at her picture on the placemat a bit indignantly, wondering for the first time who this man really was and what he was up to.

"I know, Lucy, but …" He suddenly winced, rubbed his temples with both index fingers. There was no conscious attempt this time to hide the fact that something was dreadfully wrong, a fact he had been very good at hiding in the past.

"But what, Adam?" The enchanting green eyes were on him now with laser-like focus.

"I … I … don't have much time …" He suddenly caught himself after realizing that he had said more than he should have.

"And what's that supposed to mean, Adam?" She was about to unconsciously stab her fork into a piece of asparagus, when she suddenly let it fall on the plate with a loud clang.

"Huh?"

"What do you mean you don't have much time left, Adam? What on earth do you mean?" Her eyes were blazing now as she stood up.

He forced a smile, trying to deflect, but Lucy was not going to fall for it this time, even as she wondered if she had heard him right.

"I need to take an aspirin," he said. "I'll be right back. Trust me, it's nothing." He tried to give her another one of his reassuring smiles, but he couldn't. He grimaced instead, for the pain was now unbearable, making him decide that he was going to administer a little more than the normal dose of the morphine that the doctor had prescribed.

He forced a smile as he exited the kitchen, backpedaling, still wincing and rubbing his temples. Lucy watched him as he left, more bewildered than ever as she tried to focus on her meal after taking a sip from her wineglass. She was about to tilt her head toward her plate of food when something caught her eye. It was a picture of herself on the refrigerator door that she had not noticed before. A framed photograph held in place by a magnet.

As she stood up from her chair and walked toward the fridge to take a closer look, she noticed something else, but this time on the kitchen counter. It was a rolling pin, also with a picture of her overlaid on it—in such a way that it looked as if it was manufactured en masse at a factory and distributed to every local kitchenware supply store. There were also two identical mugs close by with her picture on it.

Her heart was beating faster now. The picture of her on the refrigerator, she remembered, was of her taking a walk along the Malibu Beach—shot from behind, the ocean to her left, the pier to her right, and in front of her the awe-inspiring Foothills of Malibu. The fact that when the picture was taken had been twilight added magic to it.

However, it was the picture of her on the rolling pin that gave her cause for concern and had her heartbeat accelerate a bit. Lucy couldn't be certain, but it appeared as if it was an image of her that was shot without her being aware that a photograph was taken. And as far as she knew, Adam was not with her on that particular day. She managed to push the nagging thought out of her mind. Adam had shot so many pictures of her that she had lost count, and she wasn't one hundred percent certain if she had been with him that day or not.

There was, however, an inscription on the rolling pin that made her shudder. It was clearly visible under the thin film.

'Lucy And Adam, Forever Is Not Enough Time ...'

Her grip on the rolling pin instinctively tightened as she tried to grasp the meaning of all this. Deep down in her belly, she felt a wave of misgiving rise and assail her, which in turn brought with it its twin brother – fear. The type of fear that made her knees start to grow weak and wobble as her head began to twirl. She slowly backed out of the kitchen, her hand still gripping the rolling pin as she looked around.

At the end of the hallway, right across the door to what she assumed was the bathroom, she saw a slightly open door. The room was semi-dark, because as far as she could tell there was light coming from what looked like a candle. Lucy Young was torn between the need to confront Adam about what she had just seen, and simply grabbing her purse in the living room and bailing. Curiosity matched her growing apprehension, however, so she slowly walked toward the half-open door.

She pushed the door wide open and froze as she let out an audible gasp of horror. In the room was a neatly made bed, a dresser, and everything else you might find in a bedroom—including in this case, as would be expected, cameras and the necessary equipment owned by a professional. But it was what was on the far end of the room, the wall in fact, that knocked her for six like never

127

before in her life. There was what looked like a makeshift shrine with multiple candles burning, and also incense, but that was not all. The entire length of the wall, from top to bottom, was covered with pictures. All kinds of pictures of her.

Pictures of Lucy, the majority of them taken with her unaware and over a period of weeks, apparently. He had been stalking her, no doubt. With her free hand covering her mouth, she cautiously approached the ghastly scene, feeling very vulnerable and violated in some way. There was a chair facing the wall, which clearly meant that someone—and there was absolutely no doubt in her mind who that someone was—sat for hours on end gazing at the pictures. What gave her heart a painful lurch was a picture of her in her living room, seated on her couch dressed in a nightgown, her hair wrapped in a towel as she talked on the phone.

The picture had apparently been taken by someone from outside, and through her window. She remembered the night very well, and all of a sudden a thought that had been burned deep in her subconscious mind came roaring to life. Yes, that was it, the ringtone she had heard from outside. Lucy had just called Adam, and before his voice message came on, she thought she heard a ringtone come from outside her window. It was clear now that Adam had been outside her living room, watching and taking pictures of her, right about the time she called him.

What kind of sick pervert have I gotten myself involved with? she wondered with utmost terror.

Her lower lip was quivering as she slowly approached the pictures like they were radioactive material about to cause her great harm. She was almost in a trance as she kept gawking at the photographs, her heart beating wildly. There were all kinds of pictures. Lucy at a grocery store, going to work, taking a walk, everywhere she had apparently been over the last six weeks. Was this the surprise he had in store for her? Obviously, she was dealing with a sick and possibly dangerous man.

Lucy slowly went down on one knee, her whole body trembling with terror as she took a closer look at the bottom part of the array of different photographs.

"Oh God … n-no!" she whispered to herself.

At that moment Adam suddenly appeared from behind, as if by magic, and touched her elegant shoulders.

"Lucy, listen, I can …"

And that was when she struck him on the side of the head with the rolling pin, with all her might.

CHAPTER 14

WHEN ADAM FINALLY GOT TO THE BATHROOM, he literally fell on the toilet seat, which fortuitously had the seat cover down. The pain was acute, accompanied now by dizziness and nausea. Dr. Muhammed had warned him that this was bound to happen; it was just a matter of time. And when that happened, he was to call him immediately – rain or shine. That, the doctor had said, was a telltale sign that the deadly seizures were not far behind.

Perfect timing, Adam thought bitterly as he brought out the bottle of morphine, syringe, and a needle from where he had it stashed, which was under the porcelain sink of the bathroom.

After taking the cap off the needle, he stuck it in the bottle, and with the plunger managed to administer more than the required dose, which was by design because he was in great pain and felt that more was better. He thereafter pulled down his pants and injected the painkiller into his right thigh. He had earlier on made sure that the door to the bathroom was locked, lest his beautiful guest barge in and catch him in the act, which undoubtedly would be a disaster.

Upon managing the drug, he carefully and methodically put the paraphernalia away, stayed seated on the toilet stool, and waited for the morphine to work its magic. It didn't take long for the fog in his head to clear, and before long the familiar pull of euphoria began to get a good grip on him and he smiled. It was now time to make the best of the evening before he dropped the bomb.

He stood up quickly, but a sharp pain in his right temple reminded him that for a man in his condition, that was a cardinal sin. He waited until the moment passed, and then stared at his reflection in the mirror and smiled, made sure his eyes were clear, then stepped out of the bathroom. Adam was in the dimly lit mini-hallway when he realized that the door to the other bedroom, the room not even his maid was permitted to enter, was open.

Adam silently cussed beneath his breath as he remembered that he had rushed into the room to get his camera when Lucy was at his doorstep, and in his haste had forgotten to shut the door behind him and lock it. Inside, he was confronted by a horrific sight. A sight that made him sick to the stomach.

On one knee, gawking at the collage of photos on his wall, was the subject of those particular pictures. Something she was *not* supposed to see, at least not now, until after he had placed all his cards on the table. It was then that he decided now was the time to reveal his deepest, darkest secret to her in no uncertain terms; that he was not long for this world, in essence that his mortality was measured now in days and minutes. This, Adam Mashabela thought, would be enough to explain his weird behavior and why he had been stalking her incessantly.

As Adam slowly approached her from behind, he felt the dizziness engulfing him once again, most likely due to the stress of the situation now at hand. His chest also tightened. It was when he gently tapped her on the shoulder, startling her, that he realized his colossal mistake.

The words, "Listen, Lucy, I can …" froze on his lips when he saw everything in slow motion.

"Get away from me, you psycho!" she screamed.

The first blow from the heavy rolling pin striking him on the right side of his head was enough to send him to his knees. He saw a flash of light before the dull pain registered in his brain.

In that brief moment when he made eye contact with her beautiful emerald-green eyes, Adam did not like what he saw. The passion was replaced by something he had never seen before. It was a look of primal fear, pure hate, and anger.

He raised his hand as he saw the blackness quickly engulf his vision.

"Noooo!" she screamed again as she struck him two more times, and watched Adam's body crumple to the floor as if he had been standing on a pair of cheap stilts that could no longer hold his weight.

It did not take long for Lucy to recover from her bright red rage as she watched Adam's body first twitch, and then go still. That was when the full import of what she did began to fully register.

"Oh no …" she said softly as she dropped the rolling pin with her picture on it and rushed to his side.

She knelt beside him, shocked and wide-eyed.

"Adam …" she shook him again and again. "Adam!" she screamed when there was no response. She felt for his pulse – there wasn't any, as far as she could tell.

"Please, God, don't do this to me," she said as she tried mouth-to-mouth, mentally kicking herself for not having taken a first aid class when she had the chance, for she had absolutely no idea what she was doing. When she realized that her 'kiss of life' was bearing no fruit, Lucy rushed to the living room and straight to her handbag, from which she retrieved her smartphone and frantically began dialing. She was sobbing uncontrollably as she pressed the phone against her right ear.

When her party on the other end of the line answered almost immediately, Lucy was gripped by a new wave of panic. What if no one believed her?

She heard the voice of the 911 operator say, "911, what's your emergency?"

Lucy's tongue was stuck to the roof of her mouth. What was she going to say? I think I hurt my boyfriend really bad, and I think I may have killed him, because he had all kinds of pictures of me on his wall? It sounded too ridiculous of a story to even fly, and the first thought that came to mind as she recovered from the initial shock was that she was not going to be believed.

"Hello, 911, what's your emergency?" the woman on the other end of the line asked again when there was no immediate response to her initial question, jolting Lucy from her trance.

"I … I … well …"

"Yes, what's your emergency, ma'am?" the calm 911 operator asked again.

Lucy looked at Adam, who still lay where he was, and she knew right there and then that she had to make a decision. A small pool of blood that was now trickling from his head and onto the wooden floor made it easy for her.

"I'm sorry," she said in as calm a voice as she could muster. "I was trying to dial 411, you know, the information line. Sorry."

There was a slight pause before the operator said, "Oh, I see, no problem at all, ma'am. Have yourself a good night."

Lucy quickly hung up and looked again at Adam, who had not moved at all. She began sobbing all over again. What had gotten into her? she wondered as she recalled how she savagely she'd struck him with that rolling pin. Surely she didn't mean to hurt him. He had startled her, especially after seeing all those pictures on the wall, many of which had been taken of her unawares, but did that excuse what she did? That was just one of many questions she could not answer.

"No one is going to believe me," she kept muttering to herself again and again as the sobs violently shook her body.

With this in mind, it was time to cover her tracks and get out of there as quickly as humanly possible. She went into the bathroom and started filling the tub with hot and cold water. Lucy looked around and found liquid that when added to the water created massive bubbles, to make it look as if Adam had been taking a bubble bath. She then went back to the bedroom; it took a while, but in the end she managed to strip his clothes down to his underwear and drag him to the bathroom. Then, with the considerable effort and energy that the fear of being sent to prison, or worse, for what she'd just done could conjure, Lucy managed to place Adam in the tub in such a way that made him look like he had been taking a bath, and then stood up and somehow slipped, hitting his head on the side of the tub.

For further effect, and hating herself more and more in the process for what she was doing, Lucy smeared some of the blood from the wound on his head onto the tub. She then went on to wipe the trail of blood left on the floor from his room to the bathroom, and in the hallway when she dragged him. By the time she was ready to leave, the denim skirt and blouse she was wearing were wet with water and perspiration.

As she was ready to leave, she looked at Adam as he lay still in the bathtub, his lower torso submerged in the bubbles with his upper torso inclined toward the back of the tub. He looked serene and peaceful, as though he was fast asleep.

She leaned forward, tears streaming her cheeks, and kissed him on the forehead, cheeks, and lips.

"I'm so sorry, baby," she whispered softly. "You just scared me. Oh God, Adam, I'm so sorry, my love, I did not mean to hurt you."

She then left through the kitchen door after making sure that there was nothing to implicate her, and no neighbors around who may later give a nice description of her to the police in an investigation that was almost certainly sure to follow. However, as a bungling first-time criminal tampering with possible evidence at a crime scene, she had no way of knowing that she had left many clues to incriminate her that would be found even by a blind and brain-dead lowly patrol officer—let alone a seasoned detective.

CHAPTER 15

JUST LIKE ADAM MASHABELA, Rosalinda "Rosie" Martinez was an immigrant. Her country of origin was El Salvador. She immigrated to the United States with her mother and three other siblings, a brother and two sisters, after her father was killed in the civil war that gripped the country from as far back as she could remember.

She was a part-time student, taking night classes at Pasadena City College, with the goal of one day becoming a registered nurse. Rosalinda had met Adam after she answered an AD in the school newspaperfrom a bachelor who needed someone to come at least twice a week to clean, and sometimes cook, for $300 a week. Rosalinda considered herself lucky. The job was easy, her employer was drop-dead gorgeous, and he paid her really well for not so much work. Even though she was five years older than he was, Rosie always held out eternal hope that one day he would realize that she was the right woman for him.

That was almost a year ago. Recently she'd noticed the never-ending headaches that seemed to get worse, until he finally confided in her that he was ill. It only got worse when Adam informed her that if by any chance he lost consciousness, or failed to get up from bed, she was to call a certain Dr. Muhammed whose number she immediately saved on her smartphone.

That was close to three months ago, but over the last month or so, Adam had imposed a steadfast rule that the spare bedroom she rarely cleaned, and knew that it mostly held his work equipment and computers, was suddenly and entirely out of bounds. Rosie was not to enter the room under any circumstances, let alone clean it. When she asked why, he brusquely told her that if he had to warn her again, she would have to find another employer, and there the matter rested permanently.

Rosie normally did not work on Saturdays, but earlier in the week he had asked her to stop by and do a little cleaning, and thereafter leave with the understanding that she would get a full day's wage. Which was why that early Saturday morning around 7:30 a.m., she was at his front door unlocking it and ready for work.

She did not expect him to be awake as she entered the living room, humming to herself as she normally did. In the living room, Rosie looked around to see if it needed any cleaning before she went to the kitchen area. She stood about five foot three inches, and as always was wearing an apron over a plain yellow dress, and her dark hair was pulled back in a bun. She was a bit on the plump side with an otherwise beautiful face.

Rosie usually made him coffee at this time of day. He liked the African kind from Kenya, which she had to grind, brew, and then serve with lots of cream but no sugar, just as he preferred it. She was rather surprised when she got into the kitchen and found the table, with the candles still burning, the wine bottle and the meal still laid out and virtually untouched. Adam had told her earlier in the day that he had invited a young lady—his new girlfriend, she guessed—over for dinner, and that he was going to cook for her.

Not sure what all this meant, Rosie called out like she normally did from the kitchen when announcing her arrival.

"Adam, it's Rosie." Having basically spent the better part of her teenage years in the United States, her accent had lessened but still had a Latin inflection to it. "I let myself in, should I bring your coffee to your room?"

She kept looking around the kitchen, trying to decide what to do, but she did blow out the candles, which had burned almost to the base. What was noticeably absent, which Rosie would have no way of knowing, were the placemats with Lucy's pictures on them and the framed picture that had been on the fridge, together with the rolling pin.

"Did your date not show up?" Rosie asked as she began clearing the table, but immediately stopped when she sensed that something was wrong. She could not readily place a finger on what that was until a few seconds later. Yes, the silence! It had been too quiet ever since she entered the apartment.

"Adam?" she called out again, a bit louder this time, and waited for an answer that never came.

She smiled, thinking that perhaps he was still in his bedroom and had company. However, something—some sixth sense—told her to go and make certain. In no time she was tentatively knocking at his bedroom door, and then a bit more forcefully when there was no answer.

"Adam?" she called out again, still with the same result. Rosie slowly turned the doorknob, expecting it to be locked, but was surprised when the door opened, and was even more astonished when she was confronted by an empty room.

Everything was just as she had left it the previous day. The room was spotless save for a change of clothes hanging on a chair by the dresser, but most surprising of all was the bed. It was neatly made, and by all accounts had not been slept on – at least during the previous evening.

Puzzled, Rosie backpedaled on her heels out of the bedroom and headed to the bathroom. The door was open. However, what she saw inside caused her to first cover her mouth with both hands, and then let out a loud shriek.

There, laying with his back to the tub, with his upper torso still partly submerged in the bubbles whose shape and intensity had reduced considerably over a period of time, and the water that had by all accounts cooled down, was Adam Mashabela—eyes closed and not moving, dead for all she knew or guessed. What horrified her and made her reach that chilling conclusion was the blood at the back of his head that had smeared the tub.

She rushed to him and placed her fingers on his neck while frantically calling out his name. Rosie was about to drag him out of the tub when she thought better of it, but instead pulled out her phone from her side pocket and immediately began searching for a name she had on speed dial. When she found the name and number she was looking for, Rosie pressed the 'send' button and waited frantically for her party to answer. Hard as she tried, she could not keep her hands from shaking. The tears were flowing now, and her nose was running freely.

It took at least five rings before the line on the other end was answered by a somewhat sleepy and yet dignified voice.

"Hello?" the deep voice on the other end answered.

"Hello, thank God you're still awake, Dr. Muhammed. T-this is Rosalinda Martinez, I'm Mr. Adam Mashabela's maid. I believe he is your patient, sir, so he gave me your number and asked that I call you in case of any emergency ..." She was almost at the point of hysteria now, but the call got the doctor's full attention.

He interrupted the babbling woman by saying, "Okay, Miss Martinez, what seems to be the problem?"

Rosie sighed and said, "I came this morning and found Adam lying in the bath tub. I'm not sure what happened, but he is not responding."

"By not responding, what do you mean, Miss Martinez?"

She could almost hear the wheels turning inside the doctor's head.

"I mean he is still as a statue, certainly unconscious, but I am not sure if he is breathing …"

"Did you call 911?"

"No, sir. I thought to call you first, because that's what he instructed me to do in case something happened to him."

"Very well," Dr. Muhammed said, no doubt fully awake now. "I will be there in less than ten minutes. Touch nothing until I get there. Are the windows to the bathroom shut?"

"Yes, Doctor."

"Open them to let in some fresh air in case he is just unconscious, and call the paramedics right away while you're at it. Is that understood, Miss Martinez?"

"Yes, Doctor, and it's Rosie."

"Okay, Rosie, I will be there as soon as I can. On my way now."

Dr. Muhammed was about to end the call when Rosie said, "Eh, Doctor?"

"What?"

"I noticed some blood at the back of his head."

The doctor paused for a few seconds before saying, "Like I said before, Rosie, touch nothing until I get there. I should arrive before the paramedics do, as I am already backing out of my garage."

CHAPTER 16

INDEED, DR. MUHAMMED WON THE RACE to Adam's apartment before the paramedics. After politely shooing Rosie out of the bathroom, the doctor was able to first determine that Adam was still alive, though barely. He had with him the ubiquitous medical bag associated with people of his vocation, and from it pulled out his stethoscope. With it, he was able to determine that his patient had a pulse, albeit a very weak one, and his heartbeat was erratic.

After taking the necessary pictures with his iPhone he made a few frantic calls to the nearest emergency room equipped to handle this particular situation, which in this case was Huntington Memorial Hospital in Pasadena about three and a half miles away. The doctor then allowed the paramedics, siren escort and all, to rush his patient to the hospital with a firm promise that he would be right behind them the moment he finished tying up some 'loose ends.' Adam was in a coma, he had informed them, and would most likely stay that way until he succumbed to the tumor.

The patient was quickly and carefully placed on a stretcher, covered with a clean white sheet and blanket, then carried to the red and white ambulance that had backed into the apartment building's driveway. A fire truck, its emergency lights on, waited on the street ready to clear traffic with its loud horn the moment the ambulance was on its way to the hospital.

It was after the doctor was certain that Adam was in very capable hands and rushed to one of the best medical institutions in the country that he pulled out his iPhone again and placed a call to the Altadena sheriff's station to report a possible crime perpetrated on his patient. This being the 'loose end' he needed to tie up before he himself could head to the hospital to see what could be done for his dying patient, and to give the attending physician all the information he had on his at-times intriguing patient.

Dr. Maurice 'Reese' Muhammed had testified at many coronary inquests in the past—a requisite, it seemed, for someone in his profession, which meant he had developed a sense of what a crime scene was like, or so it seemed. So after Rosie's alarming call and the examining of his unconscious patient in the bathtub, he concluded with utmost certainty that the blow at the back of Adam Mashabela's head was not caused by him slipping and falling, in the process hitting his head on the tub. Someone had orchestrated that. Who that someone was, and why, was something for the cops to sort out, which was why he had called them.

It did not take long for the sheriffs from the nearby Altadena station to show up. The first to arrive were two squad cars with two uniformed deputies in each car, followed by an unmarked sedan from which two detectives, Jordan Kemp and Ryan Phillips, stepped out. They were both wearing suits, and their hair was neatly trimmed. There was a swagger about them that even to a casual observer would have made them out to be cops; the kind that wore suits.

Of the two, Jordan Kemp, a white man in his mid-40s wearing a dark blue suit, who was a twenty-year veteran of the force, was known to be tough and a bit rough around the edges, but nonetheless a very able detective. His partner, Ryan Phillips, was black and the younger of the two in his late 30s. He was dressed in a black suit, and like his partner, wore a red necktie. He always seemed to hang back and observe while his partner took the lead.

The two detectives met the doctor in the living room, and after the obligatory introductions were made, the two men went from room to room, taking their time, once in a while asking one of the young deputies to take pictures of things they deemed necessary to their investigation. By sheer habit they already had their latex gloves on, so that when they touched a potential piece of evidence, that item, whatever it was, was not contaminated. They took their time, lingering much longer in the room that was filled with Lucy Young's pictures, still unsure what to make of it – at least, just yet.

The uniformed deputies just stood silently, waiting for instructions from the two detectives, though it looked as if their participation or lack thereof would not be needed, at least for now. Rosie, for her part, was seated on one of the sofas, quietly wiping the tears from her face. Dr. Muhammed was close by doing his best to comfort her.

Even though it was a Saturday, he still had patients to see later that day and had dutifully informed Maria at the office that he would be running a bit late, that something had come up. He knew his young assistant, like every other girl in his office, had a huge crush on his patient, and dreaded to think how this latest development was going to be received.

After the two detectives, Kemp and Phillips, studied the pictures the doctor had saved on his iPhone, they summoned him to the hallway, where Rosie figured they could have some privacy. She could only hear murmurs as the three men spoke in low voices. A few minutes later, she heard a phone ring.

Inside the hallway, Dr. Muhammed pulled out the phone from his pocket once again, and when he recognized the number on his screen, he raised his index finger, indicating to the detectives that this was a call he had been waiting for and that it was very important.

"Excuse me, Detectives, but I must take this," the former linebacker said as he pressed the 'send' button and placed it to his right ear. "Dr. Muhammed," he said, and listened for a few minutes.

It sounded very much like a one-sided conversation as the doctor mainly listened, his back to the detectives, grunting once in a while.

Finally, he said, "Okay, thank you very much." Then he pressed the 'end' button.

He turned to face the two men who had been waiting patiently for him to finish his call.

"Blunt trauma to the back of the head, whatever it was, may or may not have been caused by him slipping and hitting his head on the tub."

The words hit like a mortar shell, but the two detectives were unfazed.

"Okay, I see," Kemp mumbled almost to himself.

"Thank you, Dr. Muhammed," Ryan said. In other words, *we will take it from here now.*

The doctor glanced at his wristwatch and said, "Gentlemen, I have to make my way to the hospital. Mr. Mashabela is in a coma, and they're not sure if he will make it to the next morning, so as his primary physician I have got to be there. Do you gentlemen need me for anything else?"

Both men shook their heads 'no'. However, in their minds at least, the doctor's revelation told them that they were now dealing with a possible murder, or at the very least assault with a deadly weapon with the clear intent to kill. In any case, as veteran detectives, they knew that to prove their case, the collection of evidence and its chain were crucial.

With their hands still covered in latex gloves, they once again went into the kitchen and inspected the table where the sumptuous dinner had been laid with renewed vigor.

"White?" Detective Ryan Phillips called out, and half a second later, a young Caucasian female deputy with raven-black hair that had been pulled back appeared at the kitchen doorway.

"Yes, Detective?"

"Please photograph, bag, tag, and seal what's on the table."

"And the food?" she asked while another deputy, Jose Romero, who was holding a large camera with a flashlight, put on a pair of latex gloves and went to work.

"Bag it too," Detective Kemp said.

Even though he doubted it, Kemp wanted the crime lab to check the food, to make sure it had not been laced with poison or any kind of drug that may have incapacitated the victim. It may prove unnecessary in the end, but Kemp was the kind of cop who never left anything to chance – he was that thorough.

Suddenly, his eye caught the corner of the white envelope under the small square mat on which the candles had been placed. He thought of grabbing it and taking a look at what was inside, but at the last second decided he would deal with it later. Right now, it was time to question the maid.

CHAPTER 17

THE TWO DETECTIVES FOUND ROSALINDA seated on the living room couch, tissue in hand, drying her red eyes one at a time. They had encountered her earlier, but had yet to formally introduce themselves. They soon hovered over her and flashed their badges, which she gave only a tertiary glance.

Detective Ryan Phillips cleared his throat and said, "Miss Rosalinda Martinez, I'm Detective Ryan Phillips, and this is my partner detective Jordan Kemp. We would like to ask you a few questions, if you don't mind. We know this may be a bit hard for you right now, so we will try and make it as quick as possible. Do you speak English?"

Rosalinda nodded "Yes."

"Good," Phillips nodded, he then added, "Would you like a glass of water before we start?"

"No, thanks."

Phillips noticed that unlike many maids he'd encountered in the past, she did not have a noticeable accent, and that she carried herself in a rather dignified manner.

The two men took a seat opposite her, the glass coffee table between them. On it was a box of tissues that Rosalinda immediately tried to reach for, but the other detective, the white one with the cold, gray, discerning eyes, beat her to it by reaching over and handing it to her instead.

Again, Rosalinda offered a somewhat timid "Thank you." She pulled out a fresh tissue and wiped her eyes before gently blowing her nose quietly.

The two men pulled out their miniature notebooks and pens before Phillips fired the first question.

"How long have you known Mr. Mashabela?"

Rosalinda looked up, as if puzzled by the question.

"Adam?" she asked.

"Yes, Adam." Phillips gave a mirthless smile, as if he was dealing with a slow child.

"A little over six months, I think. I came in at least twice a week to clean his apartment."

"And when was the last time you saw him before all this happened?"

"Day before yesterday, so that would be Thursday. You see, I normally don't work on Saturdays, but he asked me to come in today."

The detective was going to ask why, but at the last second decided to let it pass. They would revisit that during the interrogation, if necessary; he knew from past experience that some questions were usually answered voluntarily before even posed.

Instead he asked, "Who is this woman in the picture?" He pointed at the framed photo of a smiling Lucy on the middle of the coffee table.

Before she could answer, the other detective, Jordan Kemp, fielded one of his, in the process speaking for the first time. "And in all the other pictures on the wall, and on an apron we found on the floor of the bathroom?"

Rosalinda looked perplexed by the question.

"What other pictures?"

Kemp brusquely said, "The way it works, Miss Martinez, is that *we* ask the questions."

Rosalinda frowned imperceptibly at Kemp's rather rude behavior, and decided then and there that she did not like the man. Besides, there was something unsettling about him that otherwise told her to tread carefully, even though she had nothing to hide. She was smart enough to know that even innocent people have talked themselves into handcuffs, and she had a feeling that this Kemp fellow was the kind who would deliberately set a trap for her to walk right into.

Looking instead at Ryan Phillips, she said, "That's his girlfriend, Lucy, I think."

Following a brief but uncomfortable silence, she added, "He could not stop raving about her. She was the best thing that had ever happened to him."

The two men shared a brief glance, as if wondering where all this would lead.

"Are you sure she was his girlfriend?" Phillips wanted to know.

Again, Rosalinda hesitated.

The detectives, on the other hand, had a theory developing in their minds. Adam, who they had since learned was a professional photographer, probably met the woman on a shoot of some sort. The two had some kind of peripheral acquaintance, and then Adam became obsessed with her, stalking her incessantly. After all, from what they could tell, the woman, whoever she was, was a total knockout – the type any young man would obsess over. The question remained, though: how did she tie into all this? They intended to find out.

"Of course she was his girlfriend," Rosalinda said forcefully, a bit annoyed by the detectives' implication in spite of herself.

Kemp smiled before saying, "So you've met her. She's been here before, right?"

Again, Rosalinda hesitated. The truth was that she had never met the woman, let alone talked to her on the phone. In fact, the closest she'd gotten to seeing the beautiful woman in person was in the framed photograph on the table, and a few more pictures she had stumbled onto.

Sensing her uncertainty, Ryan Phillips said softly, "Rosalinda—you don't mind if I call you Rosalinda, as opposed to Miss Martinez, right? Good. Believe me, you want to tell us everything you know so we can find out what really happened. This may turn into a murder investigation for all we know. So if you know something, now is the time to tell us."

Again the Hispanic woman looked at both men in confusion; this was sounding more like an investigation with far-reaching repercussions. *Murder investigation?* Impossible, she thought to herself, but the thought of Adam dying was more disturbing than when she found him in the tub that morning.

"I … I … understand," she said, even though she didn't. "But Adam will be okay, right?"

"Oh, yes," Phillips said, even though it was obvious that he did not quite believe it himself. "We're cops, detectives, so it is in our nature to assume the worst."

"It's just that Adam is very ill, and ever since he met Lucy, or so he said," she gestured at the photograph, "it looked like he got reinvigorated."

"What was wrong with him?" They could have gotten that from the doctor, but the man had been in a hurry to get to the hospital.

"I'm not sure, but whatever it was, it was pretty bad. He would get dizzy once in a while, and was forever complaining about having severe headaches."

The two men again shared an almost knowing glance.

"And that's how Dr. Muhammed comes into the picture?" Phillips asked.

"Of course."

The two men nodded.

"Good, now can you tell us more about this Lucy woman?" Kemp pressed. "How long, according to you, were they seeing each other?"

"I'm not sure, but I don't think it was that long." Rosalinda was getting tired of the questions and nitpicking that seemed to be repetitive. Why couldn't these men just leave her alone? she wondered as the frustration grew. Why couldn't they get it through their thick heads that she had nothing to do with whatever it was they were fishing for?

"Was she here last night?"

"I don't know. Like I told you, I only came in this morning."

Kemp then hit her with, "Would you say he was obsessed with her?"

Now this was a very odd question, Rosalinda supposed.

"Obsessed? That's absurd," Rosalinda fumed in a way that took the two men aback, but at the same time impressed them. She, on the other hand, did not care what the men thought. She felt insulted that they would even dare to ask. Adam was a fine, warm-hearted, witty and handsome young man. He could get any woman he wanted, as far as she was concerned, by simply glancing at her and crooking his finger. The fact that it was Kemp who asked this made her quickly see things a bit differently; the woman was white, and therefore was supreme. In his mind, out of Adam's reach. If things were not so serious, she would have laughed.

"What about all those pictures in the other room?" Kemp asked.

She had to ponder this one for a moment. Up until almost two months ago, Adam had forbidden her from entering that room.

"I have no idea what you're taking about," she said truthfully, even though the two detectives did not believe her. But most importantly, the tears were long gone, replaced now by a fire in her eyes that the detectives were seeing for the first time.

Kemp gave a sardonic smile and said, "Come on, Miss Martinez, there's a wall filled with pictures of this Lucy woman, and a shrine and …"

"He never let me inside that other room. It was strictly out of bounds."

Detective Ryan Phillips was about to open his mouth to say something when he was interrupted by a loud call from the kitchen.

"Detectives!" It was the young female deputy, Carla White, in her shrill voice.

"Yeah, what is it, White?" Kemp wanted to know, his antennae up.

"You'd better come and see this," Deputy White said from the kitchen.

Without another word or so much as an 'Excuse us', the two men got up from their seats and went to find out what exactly had gotten the deputy so riled up. They knew that whatever it was, was important enough. This they could tell from the tone of her voice.

Inside the kitchen, they found Carla White and the two other deputies, Brian Hodges and Sylvester Walker, along with Jose Romero, gathered around the kitchen table gawking at a couple of neatly handwritten pages and a piece of paper that was inside a long white envelope, addressed to Lucy Yvette Young.

"What is it?" Ryan Phillips asked, beating his partner to the punch.

They both noticed that Deputy White, in spite of the fact that she was a trained police officer proselytized in the code of expecting the unexpected and at times bizarre, was clearly shaken by what she was seeing, and her lower lip was quivering a bit.

"Yeah, what is it?" Ryan Phillips asked again.

Without another word, Deputy White handed him the two handwritten pages that had clearly been in the envelope, and a piece of paper that had been attached to it with a paperclip. The two detectives, like everyone else in the room, recognized it instantly without being told, and their mouths instantly flew agape in total shock. A strange case had become even more bizarre.

CHAPTER 18

A NIGHT THAT HAD STARTED with so much promise, so much joy, had turned into one unmitigated disaster. A nightmare like one Lucy Yvette Young had never imagined. Sleep was elusive, so much so that she stopped trying. She tried wine, sleeping pills, and even pain medication, but they seemed to be achieving the opposite effect, so she gave up, dreading to imagine what the next day would bring.

When she stepped out of Adam's apartment, this after making furtive glances to her left and then right, certain that there was no one around to see her leave, Lucy walked hastily to her car, which was parked on the street. Her face was averted as she made her way to her vehicle and drove off. It was when she was in her car, creating as much distance between her and the crime scene with her mind beginning to clear, that Lucy began to realize the folly of her decision and the gravity of the situation.

She had murdered her beloved boyfriend; about that she was convinced, and as of yet the shock had not settled in. Maybe he was just unconscious, and someone would find him and summon help, she thought. But why hadn't she done that herself? That thought alone almost made her turn around on more than one occasion, but then she convinced herself that it was too late for that. Surely she could explain to the authorities, if it came to that, that it had all been a terrible mistake. Adam had startled her, and in that moment of sheer panic, she had struck him with that rolling pin.

Certainly someone would see all those pictures of her on the wall that Adam had taken and realize that she was being stalked by an obsessive and potentially dangerous lover, who may later cause her much harm if he did not get his way. But then again, could she truly convince herself that Adam was a monster, a sick pervert who had been stalking her unremittingly, taking pictures of her without her knowledge? He had shown her nothing but total devotion and affection; there had to have been a good reason for his behavior, but now was too late to find out. Lucy had blown it in ways she could have never imagined, acted stupidly and irrationally, and now she would have to brace herself for what lay ahead. Consequences she could not begin to imagine, let alone entertain.

"Oh, Adam!" she wailed has she hit the steering wheel with the heels of her palms. "Why, babe, why did you have to scare me like that?" Her face was streaming with tears that she did not bother to wipe off, and with the mascara she had applied earlier that night, she was a mess.

When she reached her driveway, she did not immediately get out of her car. Instead she stayed put, sobbing uncontrollably and again wondering if she should turn around and be with him until the police arrived. Tell them the whole story, chapter and verse. Surely they would believe her; they just would have to. Lucy Yvette Young was no killer – far from it. It had all been a mistake, a misunderstanding. That, she knew, would be the right thing to do.

The question she could not answer that was sure to be asked, if it got to that, is why she had fled and not called for help the first chance she got. That alone would invite the handcuffs if not answered the right way. No, she decided, she was going to hunker down and let this terrible moment pass. Surely when they found the body, they would come to the conclusion that he had slipped and fallen while taking a bath, hitting the back of his head in the process.

This line of thinking was meant to comfort her, but it did not. Lucy Young felt dirty, totally disgusted with herself for being such a coward. The cold, ugly, and menacing truth was that she had murdered a man she had fallen in love with. Thus, it was a terrible night that awaited her. She debated the idea of calling her father and telling him everything. After all, she was 'daddy's little girl,' and he would know what to do like he almost always did. But she soon discarded even that thought. It was too late, she told herself, that ship had already sailed. She would have to wait this one out.

She had covered her tracks well, or so she told herself. But then again, and not for the first time, she cursed the day she found Adam seated on that bus bench crying his eyes out, and then immediately regretted the thought. She had the choice of poking her nose into his affairs that morning, or simply walking away. That she chose to talk to him that fateful morning, and find out what was wrong with him, was a choice she would have to live with. It had been a terrible mistake, now looking back at it with the benefit of hindsight; something that was always easy to do when reflecting on a bad mistake that seemed not to be when it first happened.

Thus Lucy, dressed in a beautiful Victoria's Secret gown, spent the entire night seated in her living room, cross-legged on her couch. When she was not sobbing, she was puffing on a Marlboro Lights cigarette. It was a nasty habit she was not accustomed to, but she kept puffing at one cigarette after another just because, in her mind at least, it put her at ease. On the table, too, was a bottle of wine that she sipped at occasionally.

The combination of the nicotine and the wine had her buzzing, and her mind was reaching a place she desperately wanted to be; the place where booze actually elicits clarity of thought. It was difficult to both achieve and maintain, and very easy to overshoot and get lost in the sluggish orbit of drunken stupidity. In that realm, Lucy began to think of ways she would outmaneuver the police, if and when it came to it.

~~~~~~

Lucy must have fallen asleep while in that state, because she was startled by the loud chime of her doorbell. At first she thought that she was dreaming, but the ringing continued. She was still on the couch as she looked at the digital clock next to her flat screen TV. It was 10:06 a.m. She quickly rubbed her eyes, blinking them to alertness, and then rushed to the bathroom, ashtray in hand, and threw the contents in the small trash bin as she stared at her reflection in the bathroom mirror. She straightened her hair and wiped her face with a wet rag as best as she could, hoping that whoever it was at the door would soon get discouraged and leave. However, the chime persisted. Whoever it was, was not leaving, that much was clear.

At last she headed back to the living room and for the door, after convincing herself that she looked presentable and not guilty. Nevertheless, the voice from the other side of the door froze her dead in her tracks.

"Miss Young, open up. It's the police."

Lucy said, "Just a minute. I'll be right there."

She tried to keep her voice as steady as possible, even though she felt sick to her stomach. There was no doubt why the police were knocking at her door on this early Saturday morning.

Lucy took a deep breath after straightening her hair one more time, preparing herself for the worst as she inwardly said a prayer. When she opened the door, she was confronted by two medium-built men almost the same height. One was white, the other black. They were wearing suits, which made them out to be detectives and not members of the Watchtower. The white one had cold gray eyes, the kind that pierced into someone, and his hair was shortly cropped like in the military. The two men had 'trouble' practically written on their foreheads.

"Miss Lucy Young?" the black one asked.

"Yes?"

In a move the men had performed more than a thousand times at least, the two men flashed their badges simultaneously, and her breath caught.

"Miss Young, I am Detective Jordan Kemp and this is my partner, Detective Ryan Phillips. We would like to ask you a few questions. May we come in?"

Despite her disheveled look, the two men noticed that the woman was even more stunning than Adam Mashabela's pictures did justice. *No wonder the young man was totally taken in by her*, Kemp thought. She had the most beautiful and enchanting green eyes he had ever seen, but he tried desperately to push the thought, and many others, from his mind.

"Yes," Lucy said as she stepped to the side to let the two men in.

Instead of taking a seat, the two detective spread around the nicely furnished living room, looking around, and that was when Ryan Phillips noticed the framed picture of Adam and Lucy cuddling. She had the picture clutched to her chest all night as she sobbed, and had quickly placed it on the mini dining table the moment she heard her doorbell chime. It was a sound she had been half expecting. The detective picked it up and studied it for a moment, deliberately building the tension before turning to face her.

"What is your relationship with this man, Miss Young?" The first rule of an interrogation was to never ask a question to which you did not know the answer.

Even though the two detectives maintained an air of professionalism, they were still shaken to the core by what they had discovered in the white envelope that was addressed to this beautiful young blond bombshell.

Lucy felt like saying, *'Duh, he's my boyfriend. Can't you tell, or in your world do strangers cuddle to take a picture?'* But instead she said softly, "He's my boyfriend."

The men were still standing, and so was Lucy. Detective Kemp then said, "I see. Mind if we have a seat?"

"Yes, I mean, please go right ahead." She gestured with an open hand at the leather couch.

Despite her tousled look, so far Lucy was holding up pretty well under the circumstances, but the detectives knew that sooner or later, that façade would unravel.

"Thank you," Kemp said as he and his partner sat down facing Lucy, who was parked on the loveseat across from them with the glass coffee table in between, trying to look as relaxed as possible. But she was fooling no one; her eyes said it all. The woman knew something, they could tell.

"Is … is everything okay?" she asked.

Instead of answering, Ryan Phillips said, "We were hoping you could tell us that."

He tried to sound as if he knew everything that went down, when in truth the two men were fishing for information at the moment.

"I don't think I understand."

Jordan Kemp smiled mirthlessly and said, "Yeah, sure … when was the last time you saw Mr. Mashabela?"

This was where things could get a bit tricky. Lucy knew someone may have seen her enter her boyfriend's apartment, but perhaps not when she left, because she had tried to be as inconspicuous as possible. She had to tread carefully. They were fishing, she knew, and so was she. So she decided to tell them the truth.

"Last night. Why?"

"What time last night?" Kemp wanted to know, almost on the offensive, it seemed.

Lucy was not obligated to answer their questions because she was not under arrest, at least not yet, and could ask them to leave if she so wished by telling them that she would only talk to them with a lawyer present—which was always the smart thing to do, guilty or innocent, because people have been known to talk themselves into a prison cell in such situations. But she, like many of her fellow countrymen, did not know that she had that right, and the police always preferred to keep them in the dark with regard to that.

"Around 8:15 at night," she said.

"At his apartment?" Ryan Phillips wanted to know.

"Yes, at his apartment. Do you gentlemen mind telling me what this is all about?" Lucy asked, still playing it cool.

Instead of answering, the two detectives stared at her for a while, as if sizing her up. This made Lucy uneasy.

"Is Adam okay?"

"We were hoping you could tell us that, Miss Young," Phillips said a bit smugly.

Lucy was dumbfounded, convinced that these men knew more than they were letting on. She had to wonder why they were not getting right to it, handcuffs and all. She could almost feel the cold cuffs biting at her wrists.

As if on second thought, Kemp said, "Miss Young, would you mind coming with us to the precinct? There are a few things we need to show you."

She hesitated, wondering if now would be the perfect time to call her father. He would know what to do. But then again, these were detectives. Somehow she felt she had to do what they asked, at least for now. If things got really hot at the precinct, she would clam up and ask for an attorney.

"I ... why? ... Is ..." Lucy was a bit hesitant again.

"We just need to tighten up some loose ends, that's all," Jordan Kemp said with a reassuring smile.

166

He knew what he was doing, and so did his partner. At the sheriff's station she would be in their lair, where they could get to the bottom of this mess Adam Mashabela had inadvertently dumped at their feet, find out what was really going on, and possibly spring their trap.

"Am I under arrest?"

The two men looked at one another before Kemp said, "No, but if you don't cooperate, that will make you look guilty."

"Guilty of what?" Lucy's enchanting green eyes were now sparkling as if enraged, and the two men were momentarily lost in them.

She was beginning to feel a little better about her position. These two men were not certain about what had happened and were fishing. Only she knew the truth, and to be hiding it only made her sick to her stomach. And it galled her no end that she kept lying about what she had done to a man she had just recently found out was the love of her life—that is, until she discovered that he was a stalker, probably a very dangerous one.

"Miss Young." It was Detective Ryan Phillips who spoke this time after clearing his throat. "Your boyfriend was found early this morning, hurt really bad and unconscious. Now, we don't know if it was an accident—as in him taking a shower, slipping and falling, hitting his head in the process and falling into a coma—or if it was done to him, and then made to look like an accident. You with me so far?"

Lucy nodded, her beautiful green eyes wide with shock, but not for the reason the men were thinking. She did not hear the rest of what the detective was saying, except for one word that made her heart flutter even more rapidly, almost to a point that she was afraid the two men might hear it.

"Coma? Did you say Adam is in a coma?"

"Yes," Phillips said, studying her carefully.

So Adam was *not* dead! She caught herself just as she was about to heave a sigh of relief and smile. That would have been a dead giveaway that she knew more than she was letting on. But there must have been something about her body language, or an expression on her face, that made the detectives once again share an almost knowing glance.

"I … I didn't …"

"You didn't know?" Detective Jordan Kemp helped her out.

She was going to say that she didn't mean to hurt him, now that she knew that Adam was still alive. Lucy was about to confess to the whole thing, come clean, but something told her that now was not the place nor the time. Not until she spoke to a lawyer, at least. However, right now she was overwhelmed with relief.

"Yes, I didn't know."

"And that's why we need you to come with us to the station, give us a full statement, chapter and verse, regarding everything you know about Mr. Adam Mashabela," said Kemp.

"H-how did he get hurt, end up in a coma?" Lucy asked, still playing dumb.

Ryan Phillips said, "We will go over all that at the precinct. There is also something that he left you that piqued our interest."

Again, Lucy's mind was working in overdrive. These men were throwing one curve ball after another at her, and she wondered how long she would be able to keep up the pretense of not knowing what she actually knew.

"Okay, but can I follow you in my car?"

"Yes, but we will have to wait for you," said Phillips.

"I will need to freshen up, if you don't mind. As you can see, I just woke up."

"No problem at all, Miss Young." Phillips forced a smile. "We will wait."

CHAPTER 19

THE ALTADENA SHERIFF'S STATION –
LATER THAT MORNING.

THE CAPTAIN OF THE ALTADENA sheriff's department was a tall, beautiful black woman named Daphne Joanne MacMillan. Hailing from Compton, California, born and raised, Captain MacMillan had seen it all. Rather than become a statistic in a place where deaths were perpetuated by endless gang violence, and with many innocent people caught up in the crossfire, Daphne MacMillan had decided to make a difference.

She breezed through junior college at Compton City College, and later on a full-ride scholarship to the University Of Irvine, majored in criminal justice—a discipline in which she obtained both an undergrad and a graduate degree. Upon completing her master's program, she at first toyed with the idea of joining the FBI, especially since the bureau was actively recruiting her, but opted instead to join the Los Angeles Police Department.

Daphne MacMillan joined at the time when the LAPD was reinventing itself after decades of bad publicity, which included such high-profile cases as the Rodney King and O.J. Simpson trials that left the department with a black eye, and distrust from the public it was supposed to serve and protect. Women and minorities were encouraged to apply, and merit-based promotions, regardless of one's ethnicity or gender, became the norm. Thus, MacMillan rose rapidly through the ranks.

It was shortly after Daphne MacMillan obtained the rank of captain that a vacancy for a top watchdog at the Altadena sheriff's station opened up. At the time, the Altadena sheriff's department, just like the LAPD before it, was having its fair share of bad publicity. Racism, police brutality, and other such accusations had become the norm, and someone of MacMillan's standing, track record, and experience was needed to steady the ship.

And when the beautiful black woman took over command, the precinct was run the way one should be. In less than a year with her in command, complaints about racial profiling and police brutality were down by almost ninety percent. Programs and activities that engaged the community became the custom, and before long, public trust was restored to a level never seen before. Neighborhood Watch groups and other such organizations suddenly had the help and cooperation they had been craving and petitioning for, for many years, and not long afterwards

Altadena became the safe, happy, all-American city its founders—the Woodbury brothers, John and Fred—had envisioned in 1887.

MacMillan had a solid reputation of being a fair and honest captain who always kept a tight leash on her subordinates. There were no shortcuts when it came to investigating a case that fell in her jurisdiction, and she was known to have a very keen mind and sharp instincts that had always served her well and gave her the ability to think five, sometimes ten steps ahead of her adversaries. She believed in doing things by the book, but also encouraged those under her to think outside the box, so to speak.

So when a case regarding the possible attempted murder of one Adam Mashabela, and the strange and mysterious envelope he'd left for his girlfriend, which also contained a holographic will, came across her desk, Captain Daphne MacMillan decided to take a personal interest in the case. Too much was at stake for her not to. That was why she immediately got hold of Adam's personal physician, Dr. Maurice Muhammed, and without breaching or asking about anything that would be construed as doctor-patient privilege, the captain found out all she needed to know about the young foreigner from Botswana, now a resident in her city – most of which she kept as close to her chest as possible until the right moment.

The Altadena sheriff's department, located at the northern part of the city, is at the corner of Altadena Drive and Lake Avenue. Altadena Drive is one of the busiest and longest streets in the small city, and across from the sheriff's station is a mini-shopping complex with a CVS Pharmacy, a restaurant, and a couple of mom-and-pop boutiques.

The building itself is not large, as one may expect, just a regular precinct with a few offices, jail cells, a conference room where the deputies often meet for a morning huddle, an interrogation room, and a backyard where the vehicles are normally parked, cleaned, and at times maintained. The station also shares the same block with the fire department, and the city's Community Center, with the public library not too far away.

It was in this interrogation room, nicknamed 'The Choir Room' by the detectives because this was where, according to them, suspects 'sang' or were made to perform, as in getting a confession or crucial information pertaining to a case. The room was rectangular and measured twelve feet by eight, and had a one-way glass window on the other end where the detectives could see into the room, but the occupant or occupants could not see through the glass when inside.

Upon arriving at the station, Lucy was directed to the 'Choir Room.' When they entered, Ryan Phillips pointed at a chair on the other side of the table for her to sit. It just so happened that it was a chair facing the dark one-way glass. Lucy looked much better now. Her hair was pulled back, but the dark circles under her eyes were still visible. She was dressed in loose-fitting gray sweats and a matching top.

The two detectives sat across from her. Also on the table was a glassine evidence bag, and in it was the white envelope that was addressed to her, but for now she had no way of knowing, since she gave it a cursory look and focused instead at the two men on the other side of the metal table that was bolted to the concrete floor. The room was brightly lit and hot, and before long Lucy felt like taking her sweater off or asking for the temperature to be reduced, but thought better of it. She was nervous now, even though she kept telling herself that this nightmare would be over soon. She planned to end it by asking for a lawyer, if and when she felt the need arose.

On the other side of the glass, in the hallway and staring at Lucy and the two detectives, was Captain Daphne MacMillan. She was flanked by two deputies—James Fong, who was Asian and in his mid-thirties, and Richard Sinclair, who was white and also in his mid-thirties. They were here with her because the case had invoked so much interest in the precinct that the gossip was rampant and no one could talk of anything else. Besides, it was a Saturday morning, and as such the station was not busy yet, so they felt they could stare in with their captain.

MacMillan had just gotten off the phone again with Dr. Muhammed, and the latest was that each time the doctors attended to the sick and injured man, in many instances giving him an hour or two to live, Adam kept proving them wrong. Even more inexplicable, according to the doctor, was that he seemed to be improving. He was still unconscious but stable, his vital signs were normal, and the activity from his tumor seemed less aggressive than before. However, the good doctor did caution that this was not rare; in other words, people were known to die when it looked as if their situation was improving. However, in the case of Adam Mashabela and in light of his ailment, this was nothing short of miraculous.

Inside the 'Choir Room,' all parties were settled and the questioning continued. They were more pointed than they had been at Lucy's apartment, and the latter took it to mean that they were in their domain now and would push even harder. The detectives were also aware that their captain was watching and could pull them out at any minute by simply knocking on the dark glass. When that happened, they knew it would be a cue that she needed to talk to them out of earshot of the suspect or witness, whichever case they deemed to view Lucy Young under, and briefly huddle in the hallway to hear what the captain wanted.

"Something's not gelling here, Miss Young." Ryan Phillips was the first to break the ice.

Lucy looked up at him again with those tired, yet enchanting green eyes that seemed to work their magic on anyone who made eye contact, the two detectives notwithstanding, even though they tried to appear as nonchalant as possible—a battle they were losing, especially Jordan Kemp.

"Look, I've told you again and again that I told Adam I forgot something in the car, and gave him the idea that I'd be right back."

"And that's when you say you took off?"

"I got really scared when I saw those pictures, Detectives."

The two men looked at one another, as if to say *'point well taken.'*

And then Ryan pressed on by asking, "Did he try calling you?"

Now here Lucy had to think fast, and at the same time tread carefully. They could easily pull her logs from the phone company and see that he did not call her at all.

"Calling me?" Lucy asked, buying time as she wracked her brain for an answer that would be more plausible.

"Yes." It was Jordan Kemp this time, who had been eyeing the beautiful young woman in a way that made her feel uneasy. It was not the 'policeman look,, but something else entirely that she could see in his eyes. "I mean, after all, you left suddenly without saying goodbye. So it's perfectly logical to assume that he tried calling or texting you when he realized you were taking too long, right?"

The walls were closing in, and Lucy began to wonder if now was the time to come clean or ask for a lawyer; end this interrogation right now before she entangled herself in a web she most likely would never come out of.

"I...I suppose he may have," was all she could say.

"You suppose?" Ryan pressed on mercilessly.

"Yes, I turned my phone off before I got to his apartment. That way we could enjoy a quiet evening together without any interruptions."

Detective Ryan Phillips looked at his partner and smiled.

"You've got to hand it to her, Kemp, she's good," he said.

"Yeah," his partner agreed. "She has all her bases covered. Left nothing to chance."

Even though Lucy felt slighted by that remark, she knew that the two detectives were not far from the truth. It confirmed to her without a doubt that she was their number one suspect. She felt dirty for all the lies she had been telling.

"And what's that supposed to mean?" Lucy asked, her sparkling green eyes welling with tears again.

The two men purposefully ignored her question as they looked at her for a while, deliberately mounting the tension in the already tense interrogation room that was becoming more palpable with every minute that passed. A psychological ploy detectives use all the time when trying to break a suspect, or fishing for incriminating information. This, of course, made Lucy all the more uneasy.

With eyes that never ceased to follow the beautiful young woman, Kemp said, "I suppose when we pull your phone records at the time you say you left, and soon thereafter, we will have records of Mr. Mashabela calling you, right?"

Lucy hesitated, not knowing what to say as she now realized that she had been cornered. The two detectives had given her just enough rope to hang herself and were tugging at the noose around her neck. She knew, without being told, that now was the time to shut up and exercise her constitutional right to have an attorney present if they needed to question her further. Again, she could already feel the cold handcuffs biting at her wrists. However, some nagging thought at the back of her mind kept telling her that would not be a very good idea at this juncture of the interrogation.

And to her horror, before she could stop herself, she began bubbling inanely.

"P-please understand, I … I … I was scared. Those pictures of me on the wall that he took of me, many of which I was not even aware of, gave me the creeps …"

She did not get to finish was she was about to say, because her emotions got the best of her, and she placed her head on the cold steel table in front of her and began sobbing bitterly.

The two men waited patiently until Lucy at last managed to get hold of herself. Detective Phillips was even kind enough to get a box of tissues that was at the seal of the one-way glass and place it in front of her. Lucy gently pulled a few out with her long, elegant, and nicely manicured fingers, wiped her eyes, and then quietly blew her nose before tossing the used ones into a small garbage can at the right side of the table. She then looked at the two detectives.

Not for the first time, Jordan Kemp thought to himself, '*What a beauty* ...' but once more forced his mind not to stray. He did not like the thoughts that were now plaguing his mind with regular frequency.

Ryan Phillips said, "Something you'd like to tell us, Miss Young? Because we know something is not quite right in Denmark, like we told you from the get-go."

Before Lucy could come up with an answer, there was a loud knock on the one-way glass of the 'Choir Room' that almost made Lucy jump out of her skin. It was a signal from their captain, the formidable Daphne Joanne MacMillan. Whenever the detectives heard that, they knew that it was time to stop what they were doing immediately and leave the room to see what it was their captain wanted.

CHAPTER 20

IN THE HALLWAY, Captain Daphne Joanne MacMillan stood up straight, all five feet nine inches of her, arms folded across her chest as she bit her lower lip in suppressed anger. Her straight black hair was pulled back in a ponytail, which gave her pretty face the corporate dominatrix look that warned men to tread carefully. She was dressed in a two-piece dark blue business suit with her captain's badge visibly clipped on her left hip, and inside her jacket was the bulge of the service revolver she carried at all times.

She had since sent her other subordinates back to their posts, so she was alone in the hallway where she could clearly look through the one-way glass to the interior of the interrogation room.

It was Jordan Kemp who was the first to speak.

"Captain?"

"This sham of an interrogation ends now!" the tall, beautiful black woman said in a voice that left little doubt that her orders were to be followed without question.

Phillips said, "Believe me, Captain she's hiding something." They all instinctively looked through the glass. Lucy was still as the Sphinx at Giza as she stared at the wall in front of her. "And we were just about to find out before we were interrupted," he added.

"No, what you're doing is fishing. Let her go now, and tell her all about the holographic will her boyfriend left her," Joanne commanded.

"But ..." Ryan was about to protest, but his superior's hand shot out like that of a traffic cop, stopping him before he could continue.

"But nothing, Detective. This ends now, and I'm going in there with you."

When the door opened, Lucy turned to see the two detectives enter, but this time they were accompanied by a tall, beautiful black woman dressed in a beautiful two-piece business suit. Her hair was pulled back in a ponytail, and Lucy could tell that she had an aura about her that resonated power. In Lucy's mind, this meant the jig was up, and now she was ready to either spill the beans or ask for an attorney.

"Miss Young?" the black woman said as her subordinates assumed their chairs across the steel table. She remained standing, towering over everyone else like an exotic Nubian Queen.

Lucy looked up with her tired, beautiful green eyes that had turned red due to prolonged weeping and obvious lack of sleep. She was spent and broken now, ready to tell the truth. She had played all her cards and had been dealt a bad hand.

"Yes ... I ..."

The striking woman interrupted her before she could continue.

"I am Captain Daphne MacMillan." She let a moment pass before she announced, "First of all, I would like to apologize on behalf of my detectives for putting you through this." Switching gears, she said, "Now, let me ask you this—were you aware that your boyfriend was terminally ill?"

Lucy reacted as if she had been slapped. Jordan Kemp, on the other hand, looked like he had bitten into a lemon. His cheeks became flushed, a bit furious that the captain had revealed their ace in the hole, but he managed to quickly suppress his anger and his face assumed a neutral expression like before.

"T-terminally ill?" Lucy managed to ask in a hoarse whisper, not sure if she had heard her right. It was immediately obvious to everyone in the room that this was all news to the young woman.

"Yes," MacMillan answered. "I just got off the phone with a Dr. Maurice Muhammed. He runs a private practice on North Lake Avenue, not far from here across the street from the Coffee Gallery."

Lucy was very much alert now, hanging on every word from the captain. Her mind raced back to that fateful morning when she met the handsome stranger from Botswana, who was bawling his eyes out on the bus bench a few feet away from the entrance to the Coffee Gallery. Things started falling into place like dominoes.

"Who?" was all she could say.

"His doctor. Mr. Mashabela had an inoperable brain tumor that was getting worse by the day …"

The captain was interrupted by a well-nigh scream of despair at the revelation of this piece of news. Captain MacMillan waited patiently until Lucy recovered from this piece of shattering news. She was obviously learning this for the first time.

Wait until you hear what I've got to say next, Captain MacMillan thought to herself.

Aloud, she continued as if she had not been interrupted by saying, "According to his doctor, he was going to begin having violent seizures, which meant he was going to die at any moment. In fact, his doctor did not give him more than two weeks to live, and that was almost a month ago. He strongly believes that meeting you prolonged his life for some unexplained reason, at least for a few more weeks, if not days."

Lucy was dumbfounded as she started to tremble, and her lower lip quivered as she listened to this bizarre turn of events. It began to occur to her, in less time than it took to think, that Adam was not the psycho she had imagined him to be. She covered her mouth and stared wide-eyed at the captain as the truth began to unravel.

Captain MacMillan looked straight into Lucy's shocked eyes and asked her, "Did Mr. Mashabela tell you any of this, Miss Young?"

"No, he did not, Captain," Lucy said, her head still spinning as she kept staring at the captain in pure disbelief.

The captain then said, "He most likely suffered a seizure after you left as he was about to take a bath, hitting his head on the tub in the process."

Lucy wailed, but not for the reasons the captain and her two detectives thought. It was a howl of relief. And again, MacMillan waited patiently for the moment to pass.

"You were the best thing in his life, apparently, likely the most pure thing, which would probably explain the obsession he may have had with you—the pictures you discovered and all. He was most likely cherishing every single moment he had with you. Even when you were not around, he still valued them."

Things started to make sense to Lucy now. The seemingly endless phone calls, the conversations that would stretch on for hours, sometimes from dusk until right before dawn. Not that she minded at all, for the most part. On the contrary, she welcomed the moments, since she too was a talker. But looking back with the benefit of hindsight, it did seem unusual. Images of Adam and their encounters flashed across her mind with picture-perfect clarity now.

She dropped her head in her open palms, and once again managed a hoarse, "Oh God, no!"

"And you want to know the true irony to all this now, Miss Young?" the captain asked as she at last pulled a chair and sat across from the younger woman, their knees almost touching.

"What?" Lucy asked with a fluttering heart.

It seemed as if there was no end to this saga of many twists and turns. Adam's story had become a riddle wrapped inside an enigma.

Instead of answering her question right away, Captain Daphne Joanne MacMillan nodded at her detectives. Phillips leaned forward, picked up the evidence bag that had been lying on the table with no apparent relevance, and handed it to his captain without a word.

MacMillan opened the plastic evidence bag, and out of it pulled a white envelope. Upon closer inspection, Lucy realized that it had been addressed to her.

"He left something for you," the captain said with what looked like a smile creeping from the corner of her mouth. "I suppose that's why he had that dinner prepared. It's a pity you ran off before he could give it to you himself, and who could blame you under the circumstances?"

She handed the envelope to Lucy, whose hands were now trembling once again. Hard as she tried, she could not hazard a guess as to what could possibly be inside that was so important, let alone grasp its meaning.

"What is it?" a pale-faced Lucy wanted to know.

Instead of answering her right away, Captain MacMillan glanced at her two detectives, whose stone-faced glares revealed nothing, and then back at Lucy as she paused for effect to deliver the bombshell.

"Have you heard of the recent California Super Lotto jackpot that everyone has been talking about, and has yet to be claimed?"

Noooo! Lucy thought as she felt something inside her stomach jab at her, as if she had been kicked by a mule. *Could it ... could it ... no way ...?*

Aloud she said, "Y-yes. I did hear something like that."

The unclaimed jackpot was talked about everywhere, and the chatter was nonstop. It was all over the news, the radio, social media, Twitter, in bars, churches – everywhere. With even more bizarre stories added every day, like some crackpot woman wanting her fifteen minutes of fame claiming that she had the winning ticket, and in dramatic fashion invited a local TV crew to her house and affectedly displaying it to a live audience, only to claim later on that she had misplaced it.

Because of inexplicable stories such as this one, it was believed that the lucky winner probably bought the ticket and then threw it away, thinking it was of no significance. Now, here was the captain bringing up the subject of a ticket that, to the millions who'd heard about it, was probably nonexistent according to the latest prevailing belief.

"Well, it turns out that Mr. Mashabela was the only person who had the winning ticket and had, up until now, kept that information a secret. There is also a holographic will and testament that names you the recipient, and a few more people – well, it's all the in the will he left you, Miss Young," the captain said as she pointed at the evidence bag that had been placed in front of Lucy.

The beautiful young woman just stared at the captain, stunned to a point that words failed her.

Did this woman just say what I thought she said? she wondered. Lucy kept staring at the captain without a word.

"Go ahead, Miss Young," the captain urged her. "It's all in there. We will leave you in here alone to soak it in."

The two detectives and their captain filed out of the interrogation room soon thereafter, leaving Lucy to ponder her situation. From a murder suspect to this, her life was suddenly thrust into a category she could not fathom, and she knew this was just the beginning.

CHAPTER 21

WITH TREMBLING HANDS, Lucy slowly opened the white envelope by lifting the lip that had already been opened, presumably by the detectives, and took out the three sheets of paper written in very neat handwriting. The first was a letter, and the other two were detailed instructions regarding the discharge of the holographic will and testament. Attached to the will with a paperclip was the California Lottery Ticket with the numbers *6, 12, 14, 17, 33,* and the bonus number *24.* Numbers that had the entire state and nation buzzing, in her hands.

It was obvious that the letter meant for her had been read before she had the chance to.

My Darling Lucy,

By now you know my life story, at least most of it, but what you did not know was that on the day we met at that bus bench by the Coffee Gallery, I had just left my doctor's office, Dr. Maurice Muhammed, and was given devastating news—news that no one should ever get. In my case, the news was that I had an inoperable brain tumor – glioblastoma grade 4 – the killer type, and according to him, the tumor was so far gone that I was given a few weeks to live, six weeks at the most. That was before the seizures would begin their deadly and merciless assault.

My love, please forgive me for not telling you this from the get-go. I have no excuse except to say I was not man enough to do it, much as I wanted to. The thought of burdening you with such devastating news was something I could not bear. I'm not excusing my behavior, but I hope that explains it. Believe me when I tell you this my darling; every second, every minute, every hour, and every day of my life with you in it, is the best that has ever happened to me.

And that's the reason I felt you should be the one to get this lottery ticket. I have no use for it, as sadly I will not be of this world soon, and won't be there to enjoy it with you. Enclosed herein, my love, you will find my one and only will and testament, written, signed, and dated by me. I have checked the law in California, and I'm satisfied that this is a proper holographic will, thus entitled to full enforcement under the law. So don't let anyone tell you otherwise. Do with it as you please, but PLEASE help my grandmother, Mosidi Veronica Mashabela, in Serowe, Botswana. As you will see, this is part of my very few wishes and stipulations. No one witnessed me signing this will, since witnesses are not required for holographic wills.

Again, I am so sorry for putting you though this, my darling, and I sincerely beg for your forgiveness. If there had been a way to reverse the toll this disease has taken on me, I would have found it.

I loved you from the moment I set my eyes on you, and that love has grown with each day that passes and will continue until there is no such phenomena as time.

Goodbye, my love, and live well for both of us.

Adam

Lucy wiped her eyes, stood up, and took a deep breath. She was almost too nervous to read the will, but she knew she had to. After walking around the table in the windowless room, she finally sat down and carefully unfolded the two-page will and testament.

THE ONE AND ONLY WILL AND TESTAMENT OF ADAM LEBOGANG MASHABELA.

1.)   I, Adam Lebogang Mashabela, being 24 years of age and in good mind, in spite of the tumor that is about to take my life, do hereby make this my last and only will and testament

2.)   I'm a legal resident in the state of California, and even though I'm a national of Botswana, I was, and that is before I learned of my illness, in the process of applying for my American citizenship. My legal address is 4457 Calaveras Street, Unit G, Altadena, California.

3.)   I have no prior will and thus none to renounce.

4.)   This is intended to be a holographic will, with every word written by me, in my handwriting, with no help from anyone. It is signed and dated by me. I prepared it alone in my apartment on this day, July 26th 2018.

5.)   I'm clear minded, and in the legal parlance of the word, have full testamentary capacity. No one is exerting or attempting to exert influence over me.

6.)   I have no executor for my estate and thus appoint none — there is absolutely no need for that.

7.)   What I have is an unclaimed California Lottery Ticket bought by me at Chan's Liquor Store in Altadena, with the winning numbers 6, 12, 14, 17, 33, and 24. The ticket was purchased exactly one month and two weeks prior to writing this. It is the only winning ticket, and owned by me and no one else. The winning numbers are worth $457 million.

8.)   I have no siblings that I know of, even though it wouldn't surprise me if some started crawling out of the woodwork, claiming lost kinship and undying love once word of this gets out. $457 million can have a way of doing that, you know. My parents died many years ago, and I was raised solely by my paternal grandmother, who is still alive *and will very soon be my sole survivor. May God continue to bless that great woman who taught me to be a good person, even though I am not sure I succeeded in that quest, but never stopped trying, nonetheless.*

9.) I therefore expect this will to be dispersed accordingly, and the woman I fell in love with, Miss Lucy Yvette Young, is the only person other than my grandmother, who I trust entirely with the carrying out of some parts of this holographic will.

9.) I, Adam Lebogang Mashabela, do hereby give, devise, transfer, leave behind (whatever it takes) this winning ticket to my one and only love, Miss Lucy Yvette Young. All of it. With only two stipulations: (i) my grandmother, Mosidi Veronica Mashabela, will be fine with $4 million. Please make sure that $2 million of that goes to a trust account managed by an accountant who will not cheat or steal from her. It has always been my grandmother's dream to open an orphanage for children who lost their parents thanks to the AIDS pandemic that has ravaged my country and many others on the continent. Please make sure the other $2 million goes to that. (ii). Now before my diagnosis, sickness, or whatever you may want to call it, my business partner, Mr. Steven Basa, and I were *vigorously exploring the idea of adding an independent film production unit to our business, with the goal of producing and financing at least one feature film per year. Please allocate $10 million to that venture. Mr. Basa is well versed in that field, so I expect it to be money well spent.*

Thank you, my love, my one and only – until we meet again, and this time under much happier circumstances.

Adam Lebogang Mashabela.

The signature was also quite neat, big, and very legible, leaving no doubt whatsoever that it had been signed by her soon-to-be-deceased boyfriend.

CHAPTER 22

LUCY CAREFULLY REFOLDED the handwritten papers, tucked the winning ticket in between them, and put them back in the envelope. She then placed her head on the cold steel table and wept for a very long time. It was not until after she had calmed down a bit that the door to the interrogation room opened again, and the captain and her two detectives reentered the room.

They had been silently watching her through the one-way glass, each of them wondering how one woman could be so fortunate as to be presented with a gift so extravagant by someone she barely knew. Captain MacMillan and her men had no doubt seen some strange things over the course of their careers as law enforcement personnel. However, this one was something none of them could have anticipated; not even in a million years.

In the end, though, the captain reminded herself that her job, her sworn duty, was to protect and serve and to uphold the law. What people did with their lives, so long as that did not harm others in any way, was none of her concern—as clearly was the case in this matter.

⌐⌐⌐⌐⌐

Captain MacMillan, flanked by her two detectives, hovered over the flustered young woman, but Daphne MacMillan was smiling now as she placed both hands on her hips.

"Well, what do you think, Miss Young? Pretty amazing, wouldn't you agree?" It was, of course, the understatement of the century.

Lucy Yvette Young simply nodded weakly, as if talking on its own was now a very tedious thing to do. She was still overcome with emotion. Here it was, she was given the greatest gift one could ever imagine, and the man she would have given anything to share it with was on the verge of being declared dead at any moment.

She managed a weak, "Thank you, captain," and then wiped her eyes again.

"Good," Captain Daphne Joanne MacMillan said as she clapped her hands together. "I suppose that settles it, Miss Young. Thanks to your boyfriend, you're now a very wealthy young woman. Congratulations. I have ordered one of my deputies to escort you home. Take good care of yourself now, okay?"

The captain stretched her arm out for a handshake. Lucy stood up and did the same. She also shook the hands of the two men, and just like that, quietly left the room with a mind too full for words. There was a lot to do, but the first thing for her would be to head to Huntington Memorial Hospital in Pasadena.

In the hallway, she found a young female Latina deputy waiting for her, just as the captain had promised. Her nametag on the left side of her khaki shirt bore the name 'SANCHEZ'.

CHAPTER 23

THREE DAYS LATER

LUCY BECAME an almost permanent figure at Huntington Memorial Hospital. That was the first place she went to after she was released by the sheriff and escorted home. When she arrived at her apartment that early afternoon, she took a long, hot bath, changed into a nice-fitting dress, called and left a message at her place of work's answering service to let them know that she was resigning her position effective immediately and that she would fax her resignation letter the following Monday – no reason was given.

She then drove to the hospital, where she was informed that Adam was still in the intensive care unit, and that even though his condition was listed as 'critical', he was overall stable, and that very soon he would be in the recovery ward where he could be seen by visitors. She insisted that he be placed in a private ward when that happened. When she was told that it would cost a pretty penny, she merely scoffed and instructed the nurses to do as she asked.

After even more probing—Lucy could be extremely persuasive if need be—she was told by the doctor, a neurosurgeon named Dr. Damien Kennedy, that it was believed the tumor had initially swelled even further, and they were about to operate when something short of miraculous began to happen. The blow to his head, whatever its cause, was having an incredible effect on the tumor – it seemed to be regressing its effect.

The doctor did, however, caution her not to get her hopes up. Even though he had yet to witness something like this in his entire medical career, he explained, a career that span over twenty-five years, the tumor was still lethal, aggressive, and could kill him at any moment. So Lucy would have to prepare for the worst. He barely stopped short of asking her if she had already made the necessary funeral arrangements. Instead, he went on to tell her that a team of other neurosurgeons from the vaunted Cedars-Sinai Medical Center in Los Angeles were expected to arrive the next morning to observe the young man's progress, or lack thereof. Apparently Adam's condition, he reiterated, was highly unusual, if not amazing.

This was all Lucy needed to hear. No matter how ridiculous it may have sounded, she had reason to hope. Adam was fighting for their love, she knew, and that had given him the strength to fight with *every* fiber of his being, of his soul, for them to be together again—and Lucy was going to do her part by believing. So long as his heart was beating, there was always a chance, she told herself in spite of the incredible odds against his surviving. So Lucy found herself praying like she had never done before.

Amazingly, all this time, no news had leaked about her being the holder of that winning ticket everyone was talking about. It looked like the cops were doing an astounding job at keeping a lid on the story. Lucy knew that all hell would break loose the moment it was announced that a winner had been identified. However, in the meantime, the winning lottery ticket was hidden in a safe place in her apartment. Lucy had also made arrangements with her bank to have it placed in a safety deposit box the first chance she got, but at the moment she was preoccupied with being at Adam's side whenever the opportunity came.

Her focus was all on Adam, obviously to a point that she had nothing else to distract her. This too was driven strongly by the guilt she felt that she'd had a hand in speeding what most likely was his impending death, never mind the fact that he was already terminal. It did not sit well with her, knowing that she had struck him with that rolling pin and sent him into a coma, and had left the scene at a time when he needed her the most. This, in a way, explained why Lucy hardly had time to focus on the ticket. Even thoughts of the amazing things the millions of dollars would bring, including the diamond black 2019 Mercedes Benz SLC Class Convertible at Pasadena Rusnak, her dream car, she could easily afford now were quickly and unceremoniously suppressed.

In spite of her renewed optimism, Lucy knew that she still had to prepare for the worst. So, with great reluctance, she was forced to go to one of the funeral parlors and place an order for a casket for his body that would have to be delivered the moment he succumbed to the tumor. There was also the issue about his burial; the will had no mention of that. She thought the best course of action in this case would be to speak to his grandmother, the only surviving relative that she knew of and the only one Adam ever spoke of.

The question would be whether to accompany his body to be interred in Botswana, or if she would have to convince his grandmother that he be buried right here in the United States, and thus closer to her. This line of thought, though necessary, was way too depressing, so for now she had to fight to shelve it.

Every day and night she was at Adam's bed, from the moment he was moved to the private ward as he lay unconscious with all the breathing tubes, IVs, and electrodes connected to his body, and to a monitor with a blue screen that observed all his vitals and brain activity. She talked to him, read to him, and whenever she could, held his hand that was warm to the touch, willing him to open his eyes one more time and look at her in a way that reflected utmost passion glowing from those big, brown, beautiful, kind eyes. How she missed it!

During the day, she would take a break and head to the hospital canteen, and when she came back she would sometimes find a team of doctors congregated around Adam's bed, speaking in low tones in their esoteric language no one understood. It was obvious that something was afoot, and whenever Lucy would inquire what it was all about, she was met with rude silence – even the nurses were as tight-lipped as eunuchs protecting a vestal virgin princess.

On that third night at the hospital, Lucy got home late. She was exhausted and hungry. She'd had no time to get stuff from the grocery, she remembered, as she opened the fridge to realize that it was empty, and made a mental note to go to the store in the morning before she went to the hospital. On the door of the freezer was a picture of Adam. She gazed at it, like she had been doing for the past two nights, and just as she did the past two nights, she spoke to it. It was becoming a ritual.

"Why didn't you say something, babe?" she said in a whisper, tears streaming down her cheeks. "Why did everything have to be such a goddamn secret with you? I don't care how little time we had left, but at least you could have told me, and I would have insisted that I carry your child, babe. You would have left something of yours with me. Your seed would have been growing inside me, and I would have been a great mother. But I promise you this – I will put that money you left me to very good use. And your grandma," she chuckled through the tears. "She will have that orphanage. It will be among the best in the world, just as I'm sure you wished."

She then went to her bedroom and changed into her Victoria's Secret gown, with a slit at the front that revealed her toned, shapely, long sexy legs, and then went back to the kitchen to fix herself a sandwich that she was going to wash down with a glass of milk. She had long ago found out that this was what put her to sleep really quickly.

Lucy had a plate with the sandwich in one hand, and the glass of milk in the other, as she headed to the living room, where she planned to relax on the couch and watch some TV as she munched at her meal—her way of decompressing before she went to bed.

As Lucy Yvette Young entered her living room, she let out a loud shriek of genuine horror as she dropped the plate and glass to the floor, both of which shattered at her feet. A man dressed all in black was seated on her couch, as if he belonged, at a place where he knew she would see him the moment she entered from the kitchen. He had one leg folded on top of the other, waiting coolly for her, like a lion setting upon unsuspecting prey.

Even in the semi-darkness, she recognized him instantly, and the cold, dark stare—the same stare that had given her much concern earlier—belonged to none other than Detective Jordan Kemp of the Altadena sheriff's department.

CHAPTER 24

"W-WHAT ARE YOU DOING HERE?" a more than shocked Lucy stammered, her hands partially covering her mouth. She could feel the cold spilled milk making its way around her feet and in between her toes, but stood rooted where she was without moving.

Kemp gave her a mirthless smile. He obviously had the benefit of planning this ambush and was relishing the effect it was having on the young woman, and thus was very pleased with himself.

"Sit down. You and I need to talk," he gestured with his gloved hand.

There was something in his other gloved hand. She was not sure what it was, but from where she was it looked like a gun fitted with a long barrel, which to her untrained eye was a silencer – something that sent a cold chill down her spine. This certainly was no social or official visit. That much was clear.

The intruder's motives were obviously sinister, and for the first time, Lucy wished she had listened to that tiny voice at the back of her head that had told her to run to the safety of her neighborhood in Laguna Beach, far from the Altadena Sheriff's jurisdiction. But she knew leaving would be abandoning Adam when he needed her most, regardless of the fact that there was that strong possibility that he would be dead soon.

She must have hesitated, because she heard his voice crack more forcefully like a whip.

"I said sit down!"

Lucy did as she was told, very much conscious of the fact that what she was dressed in was quite revealing, in fact, and she did not like the way the detective's eyes were following her.

"What do you want?" she asked in a fearful voice as she sat at the edge of a chair facing him.

Without missing a beat and enjoying every minute of it, very much like a man who controlled the world he lived in and those in it, Kemp began by saying:

"There are a lot of perps like you who thought they were smarter than me, that I've put away for a very long time."

Lucy suddenly felt the blood drain from her face as she guessed where this was going.

"W-what?" she stammered again.

"I know what really happened," Kemp said. It was a statement.

"I have no idea what you're talking about, Detective Kemp, and I really would like for you to leave right now," she said without much conviction in her voice as she pointed a shaking finger at the door.

"We both know that Adam Mashabela is going to die at any moment, and what will have killed him is not some phantom seizure that caused him to fall and hit his head on the bathtub. I don't care what the captain says, you're responsible. You struck him with something. What that was, I have no idea, but I can hazard a guess. However, that really is not important, because you are responsible."

As a typical defense mechanism, Lucy simulated as much anger as she could muster and said, "Look, mister, I don't know what you think you're doing, or where you come up with these crazy thoughts, but if you don't leave in the next five seconds I'll …"

"Shut up!" Kemp snarled as he raised his voice between clenched teeth. And when he was certain that he had her full and undivided attention, he continued:

"You see, I took a closer look at the crime scene, and what I found was so compelling that I would not need an autopsy report, if and when that becomes available. There were traces of Mr. Mashabela's blood on the floor of his bedroom. These were stains that could not be picked up by the naked eye, but were visible when using UV light."

Every punch was landing on the chin, and he could tell he had the beautiful young woman on the ropes, but the rogue detective was not done – he wasn't even close.

"And what's peculiar," he continued with the smirk of a man who had the deck stacked in his favor, "is that the blood stains extend all the way to the bathroom—meaning that whoever attacked him, dragged him there and placed him in the bathtub. A closer look at his wounds shows that he was struck several times in the back of his head with a blunt object, like a heavy mug or a rolling pin, which fits in nicely with the possibility of him having hit his head on the edge of the bathtub while having a seizure."

He could tell that he had her full attention now. She was like an animal caught in a trap, waiting on its captor to finish the job.

As a last-ditch effort, Lucy said, "Look, Detective, I have no idea what you think you ..."

Kemp's hand shot out, stopping her mid-sentence.

"Trust me, Miss Young, you do not want to be jerking me around. This is an attempted murder case at the very least, which most likely will be elevated to murder. Do you have any idea what twenty years in the state penitentiary can do to a pretty young woman like you?"

Kemp was making it up as he went. There was no active investigation or anything like it, and there was no way Lucy could get twenty years. Hers had been a clear case of self-defense, if and when it came to that. But of course, Lucy did not need to know that. The plan here was to keep her off balance, and so far his ploy was working. This he could tell by her frightened, deer-in-the-headlights look.

"The state p-penitentiary?" she stuttered.

"Attempted murder for starters, which after Mr. Mashabela's death is announced, the charge will be amended like I told you. I can also convince the district attorney to classify it as pre-meditated murder – which carries the death sentence or life without the possibility of parole, the same thing the Manson girls got – if I so wish, and most likely will."

The room suddenly came in and out of focus for Lucy as she was seized by a wave of panic like she had never experienced before. The ominous words *'pre-meditated murder'*, *'twenty years'*, and *'death'* kept ringing in her ears, playing over and over like a scratched CD.. This could not be happening to her, she thought. One moment she was rich as Croesus, and the next she was in the grip of a very vivid nightmare she could not get out of, all because of some overzealous detective who could not help but poke his nose in her affairs.

"Murder?" was all she could say with raised eyebrows.

The fear was now etched on her pretty face, and this pleased the detective even more, so he piled on.

"You tried to kill him, and chances are he will be declared dead by tomorrow." It was a proclamation.

She stared at him, thunderstruck, and on the strength of that the detective pressed his advantage even further. It was obvious even to a child that he was up to something, and Lucy could not help but hazard a guess.

"You see," he continued, "you can forget the crap you fed us at the station about hightailing it out to your car when you saw all those pictures. I have the logs from your phone, missy. You called 911 right after you attacked him, and then lied to the operator that you were trying instead to dial the 'Information Line', which happens to be 411. I have it all on tape."

He underlined his point by showing her a miniature recorder he pulled from his side pocket, as if daring her to ask him if he could play it. When that did not happen, he then added gleefully, "Tell me I'm wrong."

Lucy's silence, and the tears that started flowing down the smooth skin of her cheeks, was enough to tell the detective that the beautiful woman was down for the count. He almost felt sorry for her, but he had to look out for *numero uno* in his life, and that was Jordan Kemp. And if he played this right, his life was about to change in ways he would have never imagined, and this naïve, silly, young, clueless, but beautiful blond bombshell was the answer.

"Now that we've got that one squared away, you and I are going to have ourselves a nice little arrangement."

Lucy suddenly looked up and asked, "What kind of arrangement are you talking about?"

Kemp assumed a more relaxed posture on the couch as he gave an answer that he had rehearsed that morning while shaving.

"You're a filthy rich woman now, Miss Young. I mean, *four hundred and fifty-six million dollars,* before taxes?" He whistled at the seemingly obscene amount as if hearing it for the first time, and making it sound as if it was a crime on its own for someone to have that kind of money in their possession.

"So you want money?" Lucy said with a resigned sigh.

"Well, there's an answer to that too. How about you sign over the winning ticket to me?"

It sounded like a request, when in fact it was an order. Lucy, on the other hand, was flabbergasted. Not sure if she had heard him right. It wasn't as if she was not expecting to hear him make that demand, she had guessed the detective's motives from the get-go, but hearing it was another matter altogether.

"Excuse me?" She was suddenly upset in spite of herself. This man was a lawman, supposedly, and what he was doing was extortion—something that was supposedly unheard of from people like him who were supposed to protect the public they had sworn to do.

"No, I don't think I will," he retorted. "You heard me just fine. Hand it over now!"

Lucy felt as if she had been kicked in the stomach by a mule. This unbelievable gift Adam had bestowed her was beginning to feel like it had been a curse from the devil. If she gave it to him, she'd be a fool. If she stood her ground and held onto it, and Adam died, they would be hell to pay with this man involved, threatening all manner of litigation that would follow.

"I … I … can't do that. It's mine. My boyfriend, my fiancé left it for me," was all she could say – but even to her ears, it sounded lame.

The detective laughed sardonically, and just as suddenly, as if he had cut off his laughter with a sharp blade, he stopped and gave her that dead-eyed stare that she was starting to get used to.

"I'm sorry, but did that sound like a request?"

Lucy, frightened as she was, had to consider her situation. This man knew what really happened, and if he spilled the beans, this Detective Kemp could cause real problems for her. However, what he was asking of her was absurd. A lot of money was at stake, hundreds of millions in fact. What she could do with it was beyond even her wildest dreams. Granted, she grew up not lacking for anything, raised in one of the best neighborhoods–and then a man she fell in love with, who was about to leave for good, imparted to her an incredible gift.

"And what do I get?"

Kemp straightened up, pleased with himself that he had her where he wanted, and that was on the ropes. He tried to give the impression that he was considering what she asked, when the truth was that he did not. He had thought and planned this to the last detail, but right now the plan was to keep the woman guessing and prevent her from having even the slightest glimpse into his masterplan.

It was important to keep her under his total control. She was gullible, that much was clear, because he knew what she was hiding. And if that came to light it would mean trouble not just for her, but for him as well.

"I'll give you something," he said with a sigh. "I shouldn't, but just to show you that I'm not the cold-hearted bastard you think I am, I'll probably let you have a hundred grand. Pretty generous considering that my lips will be sealed. Now hand over the ticket – *now*!"

The truth was that he did not intend to give her anything. By this time tomorrow he would be on his way to the Bahamas, and then get lost in Europe somewhere, living his life spending. He had already made arrangements with a contact he had with the California Lottery Board. They were going to cash the ticket for him, pay the necessary taxes, and then have the cash transferred to an offshore account that would be far from the reach of the FBI or the IRS–this after changing his name, renouncing his American citizenship, and cutting ties with everything and everyone he knew. He had planned it such that by the time his scheme was uncovered, he would be thousands of miles away.

"I can't do that. Adam left it for me. It's mine." The anger that surged through her body was hard to contain as she felt her cheeks flush.

Detective Kemp stood up so fast that Lucy shrieked. He looked like was about to lunge at her, but was stopped by the ringing of her smartphone, which was on the coffee table. He waited until the required eight rings before it went to voicemail. When it was silent, he strode over to her with a menacing look on his face. Lucy, on the other hand, cowered like a frightened animal and covered her mouth as she looked up at him. The detective was hovering over her.

"I'm sorry, but did I give you the impression that this was a debate?" he snarled.

Even from that distance, Lucy thought she could smell a whiff of bourbon mixed with coffee on his breath. It was clear to her that the man was desperate and would do anything to get what he wanted.

"The ticket, Miss Young, now!" There was a sense of urgency in his voice as he quickly glanced over both shoulders. It was as if he was contemplating causing some sort of bodily harm to her, but as yet was undecided.

CHAPTER 25

BORN AND RAISED IN RIVERSIDE, California, Jordan Kemp was always someone who wanted to get ahead in life. But by all accounts he was not a very successful man, or as successful as he imagined he would be, even though he was in his early 40s and, according to what was said, a very able detective. He worked very hard and diligently from the moment he joined the sheriff's department, working his way up from county jail deputy to detective, but never felt that his virtue had been properly rewarded.

Along the way, a journey that took twenty-two years, he had seen it all. He had seen the dark side of humanity, the unsolved murders, organized crime, and most of all serving and protecting a citizenry that either didn't appreciate what he did, or even when they did, never gave him so much as a pat on the back for a job well done. In many instances he was spat on and vilified by the very people he was sworn to protect. In other words, a thankless job with the requirement that he put his life on the line at all times, and no real reward in the end. As it was, he had nothing to show for it, at least in his mind, after over two decades of diligent service.

Single after a nasty divorce that took everything from him except the dedication to his job, Jordan Kemp had a champagne taste but a pauper's wallet. He was, however, a cop who believed in law and order in a curiously innocent way. He believed in it more than the public he served. Law and order was, and is, after all, the magic from which a policeman derives his power–individual power which he cherishes as all men revere individual power. And yet there was always that smoldering resentment against the public that he served.

They were at the same time his ward and his prey. As prey, they were slippery and dangerous, full of guile. He had laid down his life for the public he served more times than he cared to count, and at the end of the day, all he had was a retirement watch, a tie, and a lousy pension not worth the paper it was typed on, which would force him to find work at some private firm that would not know one end of a gun from the other as a security consultant where he would be grateful for fifteen dollars an hour just to make ends meet, if he was lucky.

Some cops were on the take, which is to say they received payoffs from people who needed them to keep them out of trouble. After all, there were still rents and mortgages to be paid every month, children to bring into this world and send to the best schools. Why shouldn't his wife shop at more expensive places? And why shouldn't he vacation in the Bahamas or Florida, Africa and Europe, like the rich people he protected with his life?

This was why Jordan Kemp was always looking for the golden way out. But he drew the line against accepting dirty graft. Sometimes he would take money from a man who hated getting parking or speeding tickets. Some cops would allow call girls and prostitutes to ply their trade for a consideration. These were vices natural to men, and an occasional extortion scheme.

However, a detective like Kemp drew the line when it came to looking away from certain crimes. He would not, for instance, take a payoff to cover up a murder, robbery, or rape, unless it was a means to cover his own culpability. These were the most heinous and most reprehensible of crimes that went against the very core and soul of his creed as a policeman. In short, he would never take money to cover these for someone else. But if he was ever to find himself in a situation where he could commit such a crime that would lead him to living a life of luxury, he would not hesitate if it meant he could do it and not spend the rest of his days looking over his shoulder, or afraid of the knock at his door.

In spite of these convictions, Jordan Kemp dreamed of a better life. He played the lottery, tried outsourcing his profession to entertainment moguls and artists. He attempted to open a private security firm, but did not have the capital to get

215

the business off the ground. It seemed as if everything he touched outside his job turned sour.

That was until he caught the case of a possible attempted murder with a bizarre twist. Now, Detective Jordan Kemp finally felt as if Lady Luck had smiled on him. And this Lucy Young woman was the golden key that would unlock the gate to a life he only could dream of.

The legal and ethical boundary he was about to cross bothered him little. Adam Mashabela was a dead or dying foreigner who, in his mind, was foolish enough to leave a huge fortune to a girl he barely knew. A girl who would not know what to do with such a large amount of money even if it hit her upside the head.

As far as he was concerned, she did not deserve to keep the money either, regardless of the holographic will in which it was clearly stipulated that the winning ticket belonged to her, and her alone. Nevertheless, this was a cause of concern for the detective, because the holographic will had been seen and read by witnesses in, of all places, a police precinct, and vouched for by a captain to boot.

The cat was going to be out of the basket soon. For two whole months, the entire state of California, and even the nation, had been buzzing about the winning numbers. The fact that it had been known that the ticket had been purchased at a mom-and-pop liquor store in Altadena, and the winner had yet to come forward, only added to the intrigue. Now only a few people, including his by-

the-book, straight as an arrow captain, knew. He
had to act fast.

CHAPTER 26

HE STOOD UP SO QUICKLY and so unexpectedly that Lucy shrieked with fear. The Police Special Glock 19 fitted with a silencer that he had partly concealed was now pointed at her. Lucy Young covered her mouth with both palms, her eyes as wide as the detective had ever seen on any one of the hundreds of people he had pointed a gun at while in the line of duty.

"Oh no, p-please, Detective ..." she pleaded. Her skin was pale as if she had been deprived of sunshine for quite a while.

"The ticket, Miss Young ... now!"

In spite of the obvious danger she was in, Lucy's mind started working fast. Surrendering her gift to this man would be a betrayal to Adam, a man she still felt partly responsible for putting in a hospital bed, no matter how many times she had been reassured and even tried to tell herself that in her position, anyone else would have reacted the same.

"I ... I ... don't have it with me, it's ... it's in a safety deposit box at a bank. If you ..."

She stopped in midsentence when she saw him take a few steps toward her. In a lifetime of being lied to–after all, it was standard operating procedure in Detective Kemp's line of work–this had to be the most transparent of all. There was a mirthless smile on his face as he approached her and at the same time stuffed the weapon in his waistband, then in one fluid motion slapped Lucy hard across the face, a blow that sent her sprawling to the floor.

He slowly and methodically knelt beside her, and then bent forward so that his mouth was just a few inches from her ear. Now Lucy could smell it clearly, the bourbon mixed with coffee. The smell was almost stale now, she noticed as she rubbed the sting on her cheek.

"Like I said, Miss Young," he said to her in a fierce whisper. "You do not want to be jerking me around. Who do you think you're dealing with? The ticket. Now!"

Lucy managed a weak, "I don't ..."

But before she could finish, Kemp quickly grabbed her by the collar of her night blouse, ripping it in the process and exposing her bare breasts, forcing her to her feet before slapping her twice more and in the process splitting her lower lip. Lucy could almost taste the leather of his glove as she fought to keep the bile from rising up her throat. He shoved her hard against the furniture, making a few items, including a flower vase, fall to the floor and shatter.

When Lucy made a feeble attempt at self-defense, he laughed menacingly before punching her on the side of the head. The blow twisted her around before she fell to the floor again. When she tried to get up, he gently placed his foot on her heaving chest. Not enough to cut off her breathing, but enough to make her realize that he could end it all with one mighty push of the leg and cave in her ribcage.

"We can do this the easy way, or we can do it the hard way, Miss Young."

She looked up at him with quivering lips as the blood slowly trickled from the corners of her mouth. His hateful eyes glowed like two burning trash cans in a dark alley.

"I've been watching you for the past three days, Miss Young," he snarled. "You went everywhere but the bank. You've been to the hospital, of course, where you've become a permanent fixture—and a nuisance, I might add. What are you doing? Waiting anxiously for him to croak?" he asked sarcastically.

When she did not answer, he continued, "You've gone to the nail salon, and a funeral home to buy a casket for your boyfriend, since we all know that his death is expected. You've been to the supermarket at least once over the past three days, and even visited a dealership to look at a brand new Mercedes Benz SLS convertible at the Pasadena Rusnak on Colorado Boulevard, and the sales person handling your account is Arsenio Sindique. You were everywhere but the bank, so don't feed me this hogwash about placing it in a safety deposit box. Now hand it over."

The look of horror on her face was mixed with that of total perplexity. This man had been following her, spying on her nonstop. She wondered how she could have possibly missed him, but knew immediately, just as quickly as the thought had entered her mind, that he was after all a lawman. Tracking an unsuspecting quarry naïve to such things would have been a walk in the park for him. Lucille Yvette Young said a silent prayer to herself. Nothing could save her now; that much was clear. She had no choice but to relent.

CHAPTER 27

HE WAS HOVERING OVER HER ONCE AGAIN her like a dark, menacing cloud as he said all this. She looked up at him, the welt on her cheek swelling rapidly and her head throbbing from the blow he had delivered the second time to let her know that he meant business.

"Okay, okay," Lucy said in a voice barely above a whisper. "P-please just don't hurt me anymore," she pleaded.

"I won't if you do as I say. But you aren't doing as I say, Miss Young, are you?" he hissed. And then in a voice that startled her once again into compliance, he said, "Now, where is it? I ain't got all night."

"It's … it's in my bedroom."

"Thank you. Get up and get moving."

When she vacillated, he grabbed her by the hair and pulled hard, forcing her on her feet. It was not a pretty sight at all as he led her to the bedroom. The bedside table lamp was dim, casting everything in silhouette. The moment they entered the room, Kemp viciously shoved her on the queen-sized bed. He did it so hard that she stumbled and fell next to the bed, and in doing so, her bare breasts and underwear were very much visible.

The look in Jordan Kemp's eyes turned from fixation to lust in less time than it took to think, and Lucy instantly noticed the change as she unconsciously covered herself. She trembled even more, and her teeth chattered as she was gripped by a new and an unspeakable horror – every woman's worst nightmare. As if robbing her of her prized possession was not enough, this man was going to rape her, violate her in ways she could have never imagined.

On seeing the sudden change on her face, Kemp smiled mirthlessly.

"In addition to that, I will have access to your house and you twenty-four-seven, and you're going to provide me pleasure any time I seek it, and when I need it. Starting now."

Kemp was going to be hundreds, if not thousands of miles away, in about thirty-six hours from now. As a parting gift to himself, he was going to rape this beautiful young woman and do all kinds of things to her, bondage, sodomy, masochism, and anything he could think of. The threat of having access to her was just that—a threat, nothing but words. The plan was to keep her compliant and quiet while he orchestrated his plan, but of course, Lucy did not need to know that.

Lucy, on the other hand, shifted backwards with a gasp. She was dry-lipped and her whole body trembled violently with newfound fear. She did not cry but moaned inaudibly – an appalling nightmare had now taken new meaning.

"Oh, no, no, nooo! Detective. Anything but that, please," Lucy wailed.

"Shut up!"

He raised his hand as if to strike her again, and that did the trick.

"Shut up," he barked again. "You're in no position to tell me what to do, murderer. I own your ass now. Get with it – strip!" he ordered as he carefully pulled the firearm from his waistband and placed it on the dressing table facing the bed, where he knew he could reach it with ease.

As she cowered in the corner of the room next to the bed, now truly frightened, he methodically used his teeth to pull out his gloves, followed by his jacket. He was wearing a white t-shirt inside, and on his side was an extra magazine clip that had been hidden by the flap of his jacket. He took this one off, and just like the Glock 19, placed it on the dressing table.

When he realized that Lucy was just staring at him, he gave her a look that told her that doing nothing would be a big mistake. Wanting this nightmare to end, and with tears flowing down her cheeks anew, Lucy could see no way out other than giving this man what he wanted. She was going to be violated by a man who society had always told her would be the last person to commit such an act – a policeman, a lawman whose sworn duty was to protect and to serve not just her, but every member of society regardless of that person's race, creed, religious background, legal or illegal, or one's financial status. Everyone was entitled to equal protection under the law. The fact that it was a man of the law about to commit such a heinous act was to her inconceivable, and yet here it was, about to happen. All because a man had loved her enough to leave her a great fortune.

Lucy slowly got on the bed in a daze, as if sleepwalking in a nightmare, and slowly began to undress. On seeing her comply, Kemp nodded with utmost satisfaction. The girl was like putty in his hands.

"Before we start," he said with a self-assured smirk on his face, "where is it?"

"Behind the picture, inside the frame." Lucy gestured to her right.

He followed her gaze and for the first time noticed a framed picture of a smiling Adam Mashabela by the lamp on her bedside table. For the briefest of moments, he was assailed by a wave of guilt about what he was doing. He was for all intents and purposes stealing from this young man who had done absolutely nothing to him. But just as swiftly, he pushed the thought out of his mind.

"Hand it over to me," he said in a surprisingly calm voice.

She did as she was told, albeit in a stupor. He held the framed picture in both hands and studied it like the way a carpenter does with a hunk of wood, or a sculptor with a rock. It was almost inconceivable to the rogue detective that a seemingly innocuous object could be hiding something of incredible monetary value.

And then swiftly, without any forethought or warning, Jordan Kemp threw the framed picture to the wooden floor with both hands and everything he had, shattering it to smithereens. Lucy shrieked and almost protested, but another evil stare from the detective made her bite her tongue.

Kemp bent down and picked up the ticket, and held it above his head as if to see if it was the real thing. He had long memorized the numbers, and yes, they were all a spot-on match—all six of them including the bonus number. The odds of what he was holding were more than eighty million to one. People the world over prayed day and night for such a miracle, a miracle he was holding between his thumb and forefinger. The feeling was incredible enough to make him shudder, but he did all he could to hide that sudden feeling from Lucy.

He nodded several times to himself before looking at Lucy. She was still cowering on the bed. She looked catatonic, obviously overwhelmed by fear. The look on the detective's face was that of total triumph. It was the look of a man very pleased with himself.

After he was done with Lucy, his plan was to take a selfie with his phone holding the ticket, thus claiming total ownership and authentication when he presented it to the California Lottery Board, then cash it and be on the first plane out of the country. He had already made the necessary arrangements for his getaway with a private jet company, NetJets, based in Columbus, Ohio.

A Gulfstream 550, already prepped with two pilots, a full bar and the richest food, plus a beautiful Asian stewardess he had handpicked were ready and waiting for his call. With this in mind, he placed the ticket carefully in his right side pants pocket as if it would break if he did not handle it any other way, and looked again at Lucy.

"That wasn't too hard, was it?" he gloated. "Now, strip all the way."

Again Lucy hesitated.

"Now!" he hissed as he took off his t-shirt.

"Like hell she will," a new voice of authority cracked like a whip.

CHAPTER 28

THE DETECTIVE ALMOST JUMPED out of his skin. He was literally caught with his pants down, as he had already began pulling them down and they were now at his ankles. Lucy gasped in shock and relief.

Captain Daphne Joanne MacMillan was standing at the door, her legs shoulder-length apart, her own Glock 19 gripped firmly in both hands and pointed at the detective. There was a stunned look on her face as she tried to reconcile the irreconcilable.

"Detective Kemp," she spat. "I should have known." And without taking her eyes off him, she said, "Are you okay, Lucy?"

"Y-yes, Captain," an equally stunned but relieved Lucy answered.

"Good, now get dressed and wait for me in the living room."

Lucy did as she was told, and as she timidly stepped behind the captain, she heard her say, "Don't even think about it, Kemp."

The detective was furtively looking at her, and then at the gun he had carelessly left on Lucy's dressing table.

"Hands where I can see them. Nice and slow, Detective," she said as she removed a pair of handcuffs from the back of her waistband.

"Can I at least put my pants on?" There was still that dumbfounded look on his face, obviously wondering how he had been thoroughly and hopelessly outflanked.

"On your knees, Detective, and hands behind your head," MacMillan said in a tone he of all people was all too familiar with. A tone that suggested she expected her orders to be followed without any hesitation. Her gun was still aimed at him, hot and loaded, and Kemp knew from past experience that the beautiful black woman would not hesitate to put him down.

"I …"

"Now," MacMillan hissed with a deadly snarl.

The detective, knowing that the jig was up, finally relented as he went down first on one knee and then the other, and finally placed his hands behind his head. Without any further hesitation, the captain instantly put the cuffs on him. It was only then that Daphne Macmillan was able to heave a huge sigh of relief.

This could have turned ugly, she knew. Though she had done it before, the thought of taking a life did not sit well with her—especially that of a subordinate, regardless of the fact that he was bent. She pulled out her smartphone from her pocket, which also acted as a radio, and made a call.

"Officer requesting backup, I repeat, officer requesting backup, and please send a paramedic on the double."

She went on to identify herself and gave the address of Lucy Young's apartment. Since Captain MacMillan was in Pasadena, it meant she had to notify the Pasadena police department because, as Altadena was under the Los Angeles County Sheriff, this was technically not her jurisdiction. But the fact that she was a sheriff, and a captain for that matter, allowed Captain Daphne MacMillan to lead the arrest if she so wished; her rank gave her that authority.

Daphne placed the phone in her pocket after she was done making her call. This time she was dressed in a dark blue matching two-piece suit, and her captain's shield was, as always, clamped to the right side of her front waistband. She did not, however, re-holster her weapon. She kept it to her side as she hovered over Kemp.

He tried to say something, but Captain MacMillan's hand shot out, stopping him in mid-sentence.

"Detective," she said. "I would advise you not to speak. You know the drill—anything you say, can and will be held against you in a court of law. You're in enough trouble as it is, so I'd advise you to shut up. I heard and saw *everything*. You tried to extort and blackmail that poor young girl. Really, Kemp, even stooping to the level of a common thief and rapist?"

230

Even though the man at her feet made her skin crawl with disgust, she still felt compelled to give him fair warning about the possible charges he could be facing. He had, after all, been one of them.

She remembered something and took out her phone again, her eyes never leaving her prisoner as she heard the first of what she knew would be a series of police black-and-whites pull into the driveway of Lucy Young's apartment building. Through the curtains of the bedrooms, she could see the flashing red, blue, and white lights of the first squad car from the Pasadena police department.

Captain Daphne MacMillan placed a call to Kemp's soon-to-be-former partner, Detective Ryan Phillips, and ordered him to be at Lucy Yvette Young's apartment pronto, even though she realized that she had roused him from a deep sleep. He promised her that he would be there as soon as possible.

CHAPTER 29

IT HAD BEEN A SERIES OF PHONE CALLS that had saved Lucy and stopped the possibility of a concerted effort at rape and extortion from being carried out on an innocent victim, all of it orchestrated by the cunning mind of a detective turned rogue.

She had been on her way out of the precinct and to her parked black SUV, when one of her female underlings—a Deputy Karla Ramirez or something, she couldn't quite place her—came rushing out to let her know that there was an urgent call from the hospital for her. Without breaking stride, Captain MacMillan instructed her deputy to forward the call to her office.

When the captain got to her office, she placed her jacket on the back of her luxurious leather chair in front of her huge and well-kept oak desk. She had on a white blouse, and the gun and holster were visible as she pressed the red blinking light on her desk phone.

"This is Captain MacMillan," she said into the phone.

The voice of a man on the other end cleared his throat before saying, "Captain MacMillan, this is Dr. Felix Peterson, head of neurosurgery at Cedars Sinai Hospital. I was called to Huntington Hospital in Pasadena, at first as an observer, on a patient who I'm told was the subject of a possible criminal investigation." He paused for a brief moment.

Captain MacMillan seized on the opportunity to offer an educated guess.

"Adam Mashabela," she said.

"Yes, Captain."

"Is he dead?" she asked with a detached professionalism that was common with people in her line of work, and in a sense cutting to the chase. Sometimes doctors were known to beat around the bush, and the captain wanted to punch the clock and get home to be with her family. Tomorrow was going to be a big day for her two little girls.

"That's just it, Captain. My team and I were called here to observe this one patient who had an inoperable brain tumor that was supposed to kill him in a matter of weeks, according to his doctor, and his mortality was cut short by the seizure that caused the accident, or so we believe. Even though one of your detectives, a Jordan Kemp, I think, seems to think otherwise."

So Kemp had gone behind her back in spite of being told that the case was closed. She filed that one away and decided she'd deal with him later. Instead she focused on what the doctor was saying; there had to be a good reason for this call.

233

"His doctor gave us access to his entire medical history after he was admitted," the neurosurgeon Peterson continued. "And then something beyond strange started happening that prompted the medical team at Huntington to contact us." He paused again.

This time the captain stayed quiet. It seemed as if she was seriously tracking the story that the doctor was spinning, even though he had yet to say anything of interest. Either this neurosurgeon had a flair for the dramatic, or he found it difficult to tell her what he was about to. Captain MacMillan, on the other hand, was someone who had sat through countless interrogations, and always let suspects do most, if not all, the talking. That was how they either talked themselves into the handcuffs, or being let go.

The doctor then continued by saying, "Because of some injury the patient sustained that rendered him unconscious, a strange phenomenon started to happen. Instead of getting worse, the tumor began to regress—and rapidly, for that matter. At first we thought it was one of those spur-of-the-moment things, for lack of a better word, when someone is about to die but suddenly seems to get better, and then dies anyway?"

This time he waited for an answer.

"Yes," the captain bit.

"Well, this wasn't one of those situations. Mr. Mashabela is actually on a rapid road to recovery."

"*What*?" Captain MacMillan almost jumped from her chair.

234

"Exactly. We're all baffled, Captain. Never in my entire career, or anyone else I know for that matter, has ever seen anything like this. And I'm talking about some of the best neurosurgeons in the world, not counting God the Almighty, Captain MacMillan."

"Are you sure about that, Dr. Peterson?" asked a more than shocked Captain MacMillan. This all sounded too good to be true. For all she knew, she expected that the next time she heard about Adam Mashabela, the very unfortunate immigrant, would be when she read his name in the obituaries.

"Actually, he's awake, Captain MacMillan. You're free to talk to him in the morning. That is why I'm telling you all this, because he gave me his consent to tell you. He's also insisted on talking to his girlfriend, but knowing that there may be a possible assault charge pending, I'm required by law to talk to you first."

Captain MacMillan sighed, and then smiled as if the doctor was seated in front of her desk. "I appreciate you taking the time, Doctor, and upholding your sworn duty, but that case has been resolved. There will be no charges pressed on anyone. I will inform Miss Young about this latest development myself," she said.

"That would be very much appreciated, Captain, and more so if you could inform her first thing tomorrow morning. It's quite late, as you can see, and in spite of what he may say, Mr. Mashabela needs his rest—and lots of it. We both know that if that Miss Young even gets a whiff of this, we're in for a long night. She'll insist on seeing him this very minute. Can't say I blame her."

The captain did not disagree.

"I know what you mean, Dr. Peterson. I will call and let her know in the morning," she said, even though it seemed as if her mind was suddenly elsewhere. The gravity of what she had been told was too hard to digest.

"Thank you, Captain, and just know that I'm here anytime in case you have any questions for me or my staff. There's also his personal physician, Dr. Maurice Muhammed, available to you, of course. He has been kept in the loop regarding his patient and is as taken aback as all of us, I might add."

They ended the call with the captain promising that she would follow up if necessary, before exchanging the obligatory 'goodnights' and hanging up. Captain Daphne MacMillan stayed seated at her chair for a long time, deep in thought, digesting what she had just been told. She then rolled her chair toward her desk almost absentmindedly and placed her elbows on the desk as she clasped both hands together, her fingers dovetailed in each other.

"This surely is bizarre," she said to herself in somewhat of a loud whisper.

Her thoughts immediately settled on the beautiful young woman with the stunning green eyes. Much as she wanted to believe the doctor who gave her the news, this was something she had to see with her own eyes. Even though it was past ten in the evening, the captain felt for the keys in her purse and was later out of the precinct's glass front doors and to her black SUV, on her way to Huntington Memorial Hospital. She arrived there at around twenty minutes before eleven.

Despite the fact that it was long past visiting hours, she badged her way through and was led to Adam Mashabela's private ward, where she was informed by the team of doctors outside the door—including Dr. Peterson, whom she had spoken to earlier that evening and was somewhat not surprised to see her—that the patient was asleep, and he was not to be disturbed.

Now that she had stumbled onto the entire neurological team, MacMillan was in a better position to ask them pointed questions, and got the same answer as before. This was, without sounding overly dramatic, she was told, a medical miracle—similar to someone born blind and later gaining sight, but on a much bigger scale.

To validate their point, they showed her a video of Adam that was taped earlier in the day. They had been observing his brain activity and the tumor from the moment he arrived. They explained that at first it was a matter of waiting for the inevitable - the young man's death, which was expected. However, the impossible happened, and here they were.

Adam was unconscious for two and a half days, one of the doctors explained as everyone, including the captain, was glued to the plasma TV monitor that had evidently been edited to document Adam's progress or lack thereof. On the third day, according to the documentation at the bottom of the screen, Adam suddenly opened his eyes. At that moment, one of the physicians produced a stack of eight-by-ten glossy pictures, screen grabs that showed Adam's brain and the tumor at its various stages.

"As you can tell from these pictures, Captain, the tumor has been shrinking considerably. Why and how we cannot tell with medical certainty, but it is happening right before our eyes."

The next frame on the screen showed a fully awake Adam surrounded by the doctors, all of whom were asking him questions one after the other. Following which they had him perform a series of cognitive tests, and others that required movement, coordination, and balance; all of which he'd passed with flying colors. In fact, any casual not aware of what had happened would have sworn that he was nothing but an average Joe who had woken up from a deep slumber.

An hour later, Captain MacMillan was on her way back to her car in the hospital parking lot with a mind too full for words. Never in her illustrious career, or her life for that matter, had she come across anything so strange. The winner of the state's biggest lottery ticket turns out to have an inoperable brain tumor that was supposed to kill him in a matter of weeks, gives it to a girl he fell in love with barely three months into their relationship because he knew he was going to die, and then inexplicably comes back from the brink of death.

She thought of Lucy Young and smiled. It was late, but she decided it would do no harm calling her. It would be nice to deliver some fantastic news for a change. As MacMillan got into her car, she dialed Lucy's number. It rang several times before it went to voicemail. The captain then remembered that she had promised to take her two young girls to Disneyland the next day, and since she was in Pasadena and Lucy's apartment was not too far off, she decided to make an impromptu visit, albeit a late-night one. And in light of the news she was going to give, she did not think Lucy would mind.

As it turned out, Captain Daphne Joanne MacMillan got more than she bargained for—and undeniably, Lucy did not mind at all.

CHAPTER 30

IT WAS THE SLIGHTLY OPEN DOOR to Lucy's apartment that drove the veteran policewoman's antennae into high gear. She was about to knock, and not ring the doorbell, when she noticed that the door was open a few inches. The front porch light was off, which was also cause for concern. Captain MacMillan looked around at the other buildings on the premises. All was quiet, which meant Lucy's neighbors were either asleep or about to be. She then slowly and quietly pushed the door open as she instinctively drew out her weapon.

The living room was dark. What woman, living alone and having just inherited over four hundred million dollars, would leave her front door unlocked and slightly open? The answer was simple: no woman would, or anyone for that matter. It was when this particular thought crossed her mind as she stood rooted in Lucy Young's living room that she heard the fierce voice of a man coming from what she guessed was the bedroom, and instantly believed her instincts that told her that Lucy was in trouble.

It wasn't long before Lucy's apartment was filled with cops from the Pasadena police department. There were a couple of paramedics as well who were attending to Lucy. She was seated on her large living room couch and covered with a blanket around her shoulders. She was pretty much shaken up, and for that she was given a mild sedative. Aside from minor bruises and the welt on her right cheek, together with a mild concussion, she was in good shape in spite of what she went through.

Jordan Kemp, now seated on the floor of the bedroom, still handcuffed, was being read the Miranda warning and was soon thereafter taken away by two young policemen. His head hung in shame and he could not even look at his colleagues, including a still-stunned Ryan Phillips. He was going to be arraigned the following Monday. Jordan Kemp was facing multiple charges that included assault and battery, conduct unbecoming, attempted robbery, breaking and entering, and attempted rape—and everyone, including Kemp himself, knew that this was the end of the road for him.

As soon as the dust settled, Captain MacMillan was by Lucy's side. She had ordered that a patrolman be posted in a car across the street from her building for a week to keep an eye on the young woman, until it was agreed by the powers that be that she was safe.

When the captain was certain that the sedative had taken effect, and her arms were wrapped around Lucy for that much-needed human comfort from her rescuer, protective like a mother hen over her chicks, she was able to tell Lucy the reason why she had showed up unexpectedly at her apartment so late in the night. Not to mention in the nick of time, as it turned out, to foil a terrible wrongdoing.

MacMillan watched as Lucy, still with a blanket wrapped around her shoulders, received the news of Adam's miraculous recovery with what looked like alarming perplexity. With wide, beautiful and enchanting green eyes, she asked many keen questions, her ordeal almost entirely forgotten.

"Yes, Miss Young," the captain had said. "It's all true. Adam has made what can only be called a phenomenal recovery. The doctors are shocked, we're all shocked; something like this was not supposed to have happened, to be quite honest." Which was followed by a firm and confident, "Yes, you can definitely see him first thing in the morning, and I'm told he is anxious to see you as well, talk to you and hold your hand. I'm told he said he wanted to explain some misunderstanding that occurred at his apartment."

Both women knew what that was—the pictures of Lucy in one of his rooms that had led to Lucy striking him with that rolling pin, and the incredible events that one thing had triggered.

Earlier on, Captain MacMillan had to bite her lip to stop herself from saying "*He is dying to see you*," knowing how inappropriate that would have sounded. However, on hearing the news, the impossible news that Adam was on his way to a full recovery from a disease so insidious, and in addition to the torment she had just endured, Lucy Yvette Young was practically dizzy.

The captain felt sympathy for the poor young woman, but she knew Lucy was tough, that much was clear. MacMillan felt she needed to tell her the whole story, instead of feeding it to her one bite at a time. Lucy had the right to know, even in spite of what had just happened to her at the hands of the detective, and a dose of good news was just what the doctor ordered.

It was then agreed upon, or really at the captain's suggestion after the paramedics cleared her, that she spend the next couple of nights at the Hilton Hotel not too far away on Los Robles Avenue, right here in Pasadena. Lucy planned on being at Huntington Hospital first thing in the morning. It was going to be a long night. Just the thought of seeing her Adam, hearing his voice, getting lost in those big brown eyes of his that were so full of passion was enough to almost forget the brutal encounter she'd experienced at the hands of that evil man.

When she checked in at the Hilton later that evening, accompanied by a plain-clothed female deputy from the Altadena sheriff's station who unobtrusively remained in the shadows as Lucy paid for her room, she made sure that the winning ticket, tucked in a sealed white envelope, was locked in the hotel's safety vault where guests kept their most valuable possessions.

EPILOGUE

FIVE MONTHS LATER, Mr. and Mrs. Adam and Lucy Mashabela were seated across from each other at the starboard side of the leased, luxurious Gulfstream 550 private jet, which had flown out of the secluded terminal of the Bob Hope International Airport; formally known as Burbank Airport. Their destination, after a two-day stop in Paris, France, was a small airstrip in Serowe, Botswana.

Indeed, Mr. and Mrs. Mashabela. They had gotten married a week after Adam was discharged from the hospital in a private ceremony at the Pasadena City Hall. Adam's friend and business partner, Steven Basa, acted as his best man. Also present were Lucy Young's parents, proud that their daughter was marrying a fine young man who obviously worshipped the ground she walked on. Already their story had broken, and had reached mythical heights. Also present was Captain Daphne Joanne MacMillan, and so was Detective Ryan Phillips, both of whom offered their heartfelt congratulations to the newlyweds.

Through an attorney hired by Steven Basa, the lottery ticket was paid out to Adam and Lucy without their identities known to the general public. Word did leak out in certain circles, but their privacy was mainly intact. And through an accountant, also recommended by Basa, the couple decided that instead of taking one lump sum payment of $457 million less the obligatory state and federal taxes, they opted instead for a thirty-year annual payment of about $11.8 million, which guaranteed that the young couple were set for life.

They invested wisely, with reserves that guaranteed dividends that were enough for them to live comfortably, with still more than enough left. $9.4 million was thrust into Adam and Steven's business, money which was to launch their independent filmmaking venture. Already two feature films were completed and having hired a very able executive producer, were brought in under budget. At present, Netflix, Hulu, and Sony Classic Pictures were engaged in a fierce bidding war that had spilled into Hollywood's *Daily Variety* after having watched the rough cuts. On the strength of that alone, the partners were guaranteed a net profit in excess of $5 million on each picture, which had been produced with a fraction of that amount. And this was just the beginning. Adam and Steven were on their way to becoming major players in an industry to which many were called, but few were chosen.

The couple stared at each other in silence, but the silence between them spoke volumes. Lucy was dressed in a long, inexpensive dress that looked great on her, as did everything else, and once in a while kept glancing at the outsized diamond ring on her finger. She had yet to get used to it.

It had been a hectic five months for the both of them. After being discharged, Adam still had to see the doctors to gauge his progress to a point that he became tired of them, but he knew they had his best interests at heart. The tumor had all but vanished, and as of now the physicians were still not certain how such a thing could have happened. No one was supposed to recover fully from a grade 4 glioblastoma brain tumor – *no one*. The disease was a certain killer.

The doctors were fascinated by this patient, particular Dr. Peterson, the head of neurology at Cedars Sinai Hospital, who now worked closely with his counterparts at Huntington Hospital. He planned to write numerous articles about this fascinating patient, who would remain anonymous, in the *Journal of the American Medical Association* better known as JAMA. It was further explained to the couple, and to Lucy in particular, that given the way the tumor was affecting its host, Adam, it had caused, among other things, his strange behavior that under normal circumstances would be deemed peculiar. The incessant stalking, the recording of her phone conversations with friends, which Adam had already confessed to his lady love about, and other odd behaviors.

All that, Dr. Peterson reassured the couple, was now a thing of the past, but what of his love? That, the doctor said, was pure, and would have always been pure in spite of the tumor. The only drawback was that upon his release, although fully functional and his tumor gone, Adam realized that he had become hooked to the pain medication. Before it had the chance to become a problem, he made the tough decision of checking into a rehab facility in North Hollywood for thirty days, and at the end of that came out clean and sober. It had also been a close call, given that the nation was now dealing with a fast-growing problem of opioid addiction. Lucy visited him every day during his stay at the facility, and their bond grew stronger. On the day of his discharge, he asked for her hand in marriage.

Also given special visitation to check on him during this time was Dr. Peterson, of course. His obsession in finding what had prompted this miracle had become his mission in life. Adam was given lifetime free medical treatment at one of the nation's best hospitals, Cedars Sinai, and each visit would be compensated handsomely. It seemed as if everything the young man touched turned to gold. Dr. Peterson's quest still continues. Perhaps Adam was the answer to man's greatest quest in life – the cure for one of his chiefest enemies, cancer.

When finally they had the much-needed downtime, the couple decided that now was the time to make that long-awaited trip to Africa. This to oversee a project that hit close to home, which was establishing the orphanage that his grandmother had dreamed of one day opening and running. Mr. and Mrs. Mashabela were going to be there the moment the foundation of the fifteen-room home was dug and the concrete poured on the fifteen-acre piece of land they had purchased a month earlier.

Somewhere above Nevada, as the luxurious jet that had been leased specifically for this excursion from NetJets finally levelled off on its cruising altitude, Lucy stood up with wine glass in hand, walked over and sat next to her husband, and wrapped her arms around him after putting the glass on the table. He reciprocated, and they silently stared into each other's eyes. Adam was again lost in those enchanting green eyes, at the same time rubbing his cheek against hers, feeling the velvety softness of her skin and wondering how someone could possibly be this beautiful, never missing the opportunity to tell her that.

They stayed that way for hours until they fell into a deep sleep, after making love on the long leather couch. Paris, the city of love, was still another eight or ten hours away. And then after that it would be off to Botswana, and the village of Serowe to be exact, where an anxious grandmother waited to hold in her arms a grandson she loved more than anything else in this world, and also to meet the granddaughter-in-law she had heard so much about.

THE END

AUTHOR'S NOTE

THIS INDEED IS A WORK OF FICTION, and more so than usual. Almost nothing in the previous two hundred and forty-odd pages is based on reality. Research, hardly a priority, was rarely called upon; accuracy, especially in all things considered medical, was not deemed crucial. Long paragraphs of fiction were used to avoid looking up facts. I do not know anyone suffering from an inoperable brain tumor (Thank God), and as of yet I do not know of anyone who has fully recovered from one, but I sincerely hope the cure for cancer will be realized during our lifetime. Save for known locales that were used fictionally, none of what is described in "*IRONIC*" ever happened to anyone I know of or heard of; and I don't personally know anyone who has won the California State Lottery yet. It was all a product of my imagination.